Nasty, Short and Brutal

T0159784

NASTY, SHORT AND BRUTAL

Daniel Nemiroff

TORONTO

Exile Editions
2004

First published in Canada in 2004 by
Exile Editions Ltd.
20 Dale Avenue
Toronto, Ontario, M4W 1K4
telephone: 416 485 9468
www.ExileEditions.com

Library and Archives Canada Cataloguing in Publication

Nemiroff, Daniel, 1968-
    Nasty, short and brutal / Daniel Nemiroff.

Short stories.
ISBN 1-55096-609-X

    I. Title.

PS8627.E59N27 2005   C813'.6   C2005-905253-8

Design and Composition: Michael P.M. Callaghan
Typesetting: Moons of Jupiter
Printed in Canada by: Gauvin Imprimerie

The publisher would like to acknowledge the financial assistance of
The Canada Council for the Arts.

The Canada Council Le Conseil des Arts
FOR THE ARTS   DU CANADA
SINCE 1957   DEPUIS 1957

10 9 8 7 6 5 4 3 2 1

BATTING ORDER

ARCH ANGELS

*G*abe parks the Mercedes in the alley behind Raef's apartment. He'd
had no trouble finding the place, didn't even consult the map his sister had thoughtfully left in the glove compartment. The whole city had
come back to him in a flash. It always did, wherever he went, if he'd been
there at least once before. That's just the way his mind works. For example, the last time he'd been in Winnipeg, four years earlier, he'd noticed
that the A&W had moved from one side of Osborne to the other. This time
he'd taken a smarter approach into town, circumnavigating downtown by
continuing on the road to Brandon, then turning onto the Pembina
Highway. Unfortunately, this route didn't allow him to see if A&W had
changed locations or stayed put. He'd have to check on it later.

The back of the building is exactly as Gabe remembers it. He grabs
his overnight bag, leaving the major luggage in the trunk, and flies up the
stairs. He is on the third-floor landing in no time flat. He glances into the
apartment next to Raef's and wonders if Arielle still lives there. If so,
she'd redone her kitchen. He liked it the way it was before — gleaming
white surfaces, chrome fixtures, no curtains to obstruct the natural light.

The screen door leading to Raef's kitchen is propped open by an
unhealthy potted tomato plant. There are two dishes in the sink, two more
on the counter. Gabe hears the dull hum of a television set, its volume
turned all the way down, and something resembling human speech coming from the living room.

Raef is huddled on the far end of the couch, the only corner not bathed
in the evening sunlight. He has an extinguished joint in his hand and his
face is expressionless.

"Hey," Raef says, not looking up, not looking for a light, not looking at the TV, not really looking at anything, "I didn't think you were coming until tomorrow."

"I drove straight through. Didn't think I had it in me anymore . . . but here I am."

"Thirty hours?"

"Thirty-two. It was a bitch getting out of Toronto."

"It always is."

Gabe wants to get the whole thing off his chest: why he's moving to Vancouver, how his sister's fascist husband had given him 10 days and 200 bucks to get the car to their palatial spread in West Van, the injustice he's had to deal with, not just at work, but all the crap with his landlord and the union . . . He'd busted his hump to get to Winnipeg just to have this conversation with Raef, but he doesn't.

"You smoking again?" Gabe asks, nodding towards the half-cigarette in the art-deco ashtray standing between the couch and the La-Z-Boy.

"No tobacco for me. Mike's here."

"I don't think he'd mind . . ." Gabe says, taking the butt from the ash-tray and lighting it with the last match in a pack he'd picked up at a Husky station outside of Thunder Bay.

"I thought you quit."

"You try driving across Ontario without nicotine."

Mike comes out of the bathroom, gives Gabe a look of faint recognition, almost nods and settles himself into the La-Z-Boy, the only other seat in the room not scorched by the Prairie sun. He pulls a cigarette from his breast pocket, straight from the heart, the way they all used to do it. He lights the smoke with one fluid motion of his golden Zippo.

The words "PRESS ANY BUTTON" flash alternately in various corners of the TV screen. The three of them are staring at it, transfixed. Gabe feels like he should be feeling something; glad to see his friends, tired from the long drive, a little put off by the dishes in the sink . . . but he doesn't. He doesn't feel anything.

Mike puts his cigarette out after three drags and shifts in the La-Z-Boy as the sun encroaches over the shoulder of his chair. They continue to stare at the screen. Gabe wonders if there is a pattern to where the words "PRESS ANY BUTTON" will appear. Top left, centre right, top right, top right again with a slight over-lap, dead centre . . . is that what they're doing, trying to find some meaning in the randomness? Is there some astrological significance to be divined from the digital screen? Could there really be some indication of a higher order or intelligence hidden in those three promising words?

Try as he might, Gabe can't detect the pattern. He finally asks, "What time does the sun go down?"

"10 o'clock . . . if we're lucky," Raef answers, nudging himself further from the light.

"That's . . ."

"Depressing."

They leave it at that for the moment. The moment drags. Gabe shuffles his feet, tries looking out the window, but finds his gaze returning to the television. He is again transfixed by the flashing logo.

Mike finally says, "How was the drive?"

"It was like someone was shooting at my windshield with an insect machine gun." Gabe had prepared the joke while scrubbing dead bugs off the hood of the Mercedes in the hospitality centre on the Trans-Canada, just past Marathon, Ontario, 26.2 miles to nowhere any direction you go. He keeps that one to himself. "You really get a sense of how grotesquely underpopulated this country is. We could throw 30 million Chinese into Northern Ontario, give 'em each 40 acres and a John Deere, not hear from them for 20 years and oh, what a society they'd build."

The joke falls flat.

A million molecules of dust dance in the sunlight.

"PRESS ANY BUTTON" flashes on the screen, bottom left.

"The spare room is a bit of a disaster," Raef says out of nowhere, waving vaguely towards the back of the apartment. "But, you know, make yourself at home."

Raef wasn't exaggerating. The floor is littered with an odd assortment of newspapers, old magazines, Raef's personal papers, an old tax return, his high-school transcripts, various notes from medical journals . . .The futon, the same one Gabe slept on the last time he'd been in town four years earlier, the one with the metal bar down the middle, had become an extension of the floor. The mountain of papers that start by the desk and rise in perfect correspondence with the grade of the bed turn out to be the broadsheets of an advanced microbiology textbook Raef had edited. Gabe remembers this one. It had caused Raef so much grief he'd hired Arielle to help him. Gabe had been both jealous of and hopeful for his friend. There was just something about her . . .

Gabe carefully removes the stacks of paper from the bed and places them on the floor. He sweeps sand and dust from the sheet, the same one he'd used the last time, probably the same sand he'd left behind after their day trip to Grand beach, and unfolds the couch into a bed.

By the time Gabe gets back to the living room, some three minutes later, Mike is gone. "Did I do something?" Gabe asks, settling himself into the vacated La-Z-Boy.

"Mike's got his own demons to fight."

"Well, at least he left me a smoke." Gabe takes the barely smoked cigarette from the ashtray and lets his eyes wander over the coffee table, resting them on the little plastic baggie and fancy rolling papers in front of Raef. "Although a man can't survive on nicotine alone . . ."

"Go ahead, mi dope es su dope."

Gabe breaks off a third of the partially smoked cigarette, crumbles the tobacco and marijuana together, and using a strip of the defunct Husky-station matchbook as a filter, rolls an expert joint, despite not having smoked for years. "How can a high-school drug counsellor get away with toking up?" he used to say. Make that an ex-high-school drug counsellor. He wants to discuss his dismissal with someone and who better than Raef? We could get into how the stupid Tory government, with their rural power base and narrow-minded fiscal conservatism, decided schools in urban Toronto didn't need drug prevention programs since all the small town/suburban kids seemed to do just fine without them, thank you very much. The bastards even overrode the Board of School Trustees, an elected body in their own right . . . and his union rep didn't want to hear boo about it . . . What the hell, Gabe thinks, taking in the first long, heavy drag. Raef doesn't need to hear it and I can't talk about it anymore.

"That's not good," Raef comments, relighting his joint and passing the lighter over to Gabe. "Tobacco in a joint is bad enough, but that's . . ."

"The only relief I've had in recent memory. What's Mike's problem?"

"His career, his kid, death in the family, life in the family . . ."

"Something happen to Ike?"

"You know, Ike's not really his kid, right? He's his stepson. Last year, out of nowhere, Real Dad comes back and demands access to his only begotten. The thing is, Mike had already split-up with Ike's mom, but still spent time with the kid, treated him like his own. The other thing is Real Dad isn't interested in the kid, he just wants to burn Mike and the ex. Anyhow, Mike can't leave it alone and the ex tells him Real Dad is an abuser, which is why she left him in the first place. Mike sees Ike in the street and the kid's got a black eye. Now, Ike never said that his father had hurt him, never said anything . . . But Mike goes over to Real Dad's place and kicks his ass something serious."

"You don't want to piss Mike off . . ."

"No, you don't."

"So, why is he still pissed off?"

"Now the kid won't talk to him at all."

"Can I ask you something," Gabe says, leaning in, watching his smoke curl through the incessant sunbeam. "Is this really the best thing on TV?"

"It's the only thing on TV. I cancelled my cable three months ago."

"Yeah?"

"I'd sit down at 8 o'clock, start flipping around, not find anything, keep flipping, still not watching anything, and next thing you know it's four in the morning and I've wasted the whole night."

"That's the nature of the beast . . . I don't even have a TV anymore. I sold it along with almost everything else I owned. All I've got left is in the trunk of my brother-in-law's car out back."

They smoke in silence for a few moments, digesting their mutual and sudden turn towards minimalism. When they finally speak it is in a familiar yet distancing shorthand of word and miniscule gesture. Two old friends. They stare at the flashing icon for twenty minutes . . . an eternity before Gabe speaks. "Anything?"

"A nine-thirty?"

"Calls?" Gabe raises his eyebrow.

Raef's eyes circle once for "No" and once for "You want to drive?"

"Two straight days . . ." Gabe exhales.

"Keys . . ." Raef says, inaudible but to himself, running his fingers over his pockets.

The last time Gabe was in Raef's car they'd taken an all back-streets route, going as fast as the old Lincoln could fly. They made half-hearted yields at stop signs to the Donald Street bridge and a straight shot to Portage Place, then went around the back to the almost gentrified little laneway between the shopping mall and the adjacent high-rise condos that had gone up between Gabe's last visit and the one before. He remembers telling Raef how Winnipeg always felt like a time warp to him. "It's like the town never got out of 1935. It feels like the Great Depression is still going on. I think it's the architecture. I mean the people are so friendly—"

"You're wrong, it is the people, or the underlying spirit of the people," Raef put in. "I've been here 10 years and a hundred winters and I still don't believe it."

"What, the friendliness?"

"It's all propaganda. They stamp it on the licence plates and everyone starts believing it. Deep down they're just like everyone else."

Their conversation had been animated that day. Raef was in a good mood: he'd received a new contract, nearly six months' worth of work which, given his rates and lifestyle, would support him for a year and a half, maybe even two years. "That's the way it is in this business," he'd said in that happy/bitter way of his.

Gabe didn't point out that Raef had chosen his own path, had decided all by himself to be a doctor who would not see a patient, do a residency, use his natural gifts for the benefit of mankind. If Raef wanted to edit medical texts, let him. If he wants to be cut off from humanity, from himself, that's his right. Who was Gabe to talk . . . at least he was helping people back then. Now though, now Gabe is directionless, watching the back streets of Winnipeg fly by.

The last time they went downtown, four years ago, they were early for the show they were going to and went cruising through the Exchange. Gabe was chatted-up by a very young, very blonde hooker for a good ten minutes before he finally refused her services. The show was good; at least Gabe thought so at the time. It was a new play by an old friend (possibly ex-lover?) of Raef's then quasi-girlfriend Martha. They'd all gone out to some bookstore-come-bar around the corner and made quite the night of it. Gabe had liked everyone there, and not just for their classic Manitoban friendliness. He'd found them interesting and, more importantly, real. He embarked, as he often does, on a long, fairly shaky social theory based on the basic (pre-Pauline) Christian ethic as embodied by the good people of the Peg. He was a big hit with the locals, and Raef, to his credit, helped pump him up, actually laughing along with the others, telling stories of those days of yore when they were young, wild, and thought themselves free.

Gabe had to admit to himself he got a thrill from playing the part of the street-wise prophet from the big bad East, and from the ego massage Raef had given him. When Gabe spoke, they had listened.

The silence in the car is a continuation of the silence in the apartment, only without the encroaching sun and flashing invitation to "PRESS ANY BUTTON." This time their route is even more obscure. Raef had discovered new back streets and is taking a different bridge. Gabe is about to comment, say something about checking on the A&W, but his words are swallowed by the humming of the big Lincoln. Instead, he concentrates on remembering that party, placing names to faces in his mind's eye, tiny mug shots of structured imagination. Maybe Gabe will see some of them while he's in town. There should be plenty of time to get something together, maybe tomorrow night . . . Friday? Saturday is possible if he's willing to drive straight from Winnipeg to Calgary . . . That might not be necessary. The one he wants to see, is seeing in his mind, is Raef's neighbour Arielle. Arielle, who may or may not still live next door, who may or may not have remodelled her kitchen. Raef had said that he had a thing for her, but she knew better, knew that Raef wasn't offering what she wanted — stability, marriage, children. Gabe had fallen for her too, but as always he was just passing through and couldn't offer her what she wanted either . . . especially since he was in a sorta-relationship at the time with Sara . . . or was it Esther then? It didn't matter. He'd have dumped either of them for Arielle in a heartbeat.

What was it about her, Gabe wonders, leaning hard into the door as Raef rounds a corner full-steam. It's that she's one of us. In that one night, four years ago, it had been clear that Arielle was in the inner circle of old friends, friends who'd known each other since before time began, just by virtue of being who she was. Is. She knew the language and the mind-set, read their communion of gesture and returned it in kind. When the party was over it was just the four of them; Mike, Raef, Gabe and Arielle back at Raef's place. She'd gone to work on the kitchen, made it shine, while they retired to the living room, allegedly to pick up the empty bottles.

When she was done, Arielle found the three boys smoking a joint, bottles still on the floor, Raef slouching on the couch, Mike in the La-Z-Boy, and Gabe standing at the far side of the table, shuffling his feet. She just smiled, stood in front of the TV set and took the joint Gabe passed her. After two quick tokes, she lit the room up with her smile and went home. They had all seen it. They had all felt it . . . that light that came from her.

This time Raef approaches Portage Place from the other side and parks by the back doors. They are right around the corner from where they'd parked the last time. Raef turns off the ignition, and after three attempts successfully relights his joint. Gabe quashes a sudden impulse to interrupt the silence by trying out his new pet theory, the one he plans to launch into if there should be a social gathering of some sort while he's in town. But why would Raef give a damn about the Yogurt Integration Doctrine? Why would anyone? Despite the hopeful message, i.e.: the North American acceptance of yogurt as a common household product sometime in the late 1970s to early 1980s, which led to Greek, Indian, and Lebanese restaurants becoming more mainstream, even de-ghettoized, particularly in the urban centres, leading to more inter-cultural contact, hence world peace . . . Gabe knows it to be nonsense and not even that funny. Any passion he had for it dissipates before it touches the air.

Raef puts out the remains of the roach and waits for Gabe to get out so that he can lock the door. Gabe scoots around the back of the big car, tracing its tail fin with his finger. With his other hand he digs in his pocket for parking-meter change. Raef kick-slams the driver's side door closed behind him and pats his pockets for the keys he's left dangling in the ignition.

"You have to pay until 10 . . . maybe they validate inside."

"Uhhh . . ."

Gabe turns to his friend. He follows the line of his gaze to the keys in the ignition and instantly deduces their dilemma and its inevitable conclusion: no matter how friendly a city is, you can't just leave your keys in the ignition or bad things will happen. Why place temptation before the weak? It's cruel. Gabe has seen it a thousand times and it never fails to break his heart.

Raef disappears into the mall in search of a wire hanger, a security guard, a telephone . . . Gabe isn't sure. He'd silently volunteered to watch over the car, lean against the hood looking cool, invisible, observing the world — the three teenage boys skateboarding down the handicapped ramp, the family of fat Cree waiting by the doors for a ride, or maybe just waiting for nothing. There was a time, not so long ago on the cosmic scale, when Gabe would have walked right up to them, any of them, the skateboarders, the Natives, or the four young Mennonite girls now coming around the corner.

The old Gabe, the one with the job, the purpose, the message, could find his way with any of them. He had confidence and didn't have to think before he spoke; it all just seemed to flow through him and from him. And it worked. He had reached people. But had he? Really? How long did his effect linger? That was the question. How many teenaged addicts had the great Gabriel actually cured? How many had he just steered into an addiction to the Twelve Steps and all they represent? How many had he failed with completely . . . and here he is, stoned for the first time in years and not even feeling guilty about it. He is glad of it. He hopes to do it again soon. For him the world is glowing, its centre is one of the young Mennonite girls. He wants to approach her . . .

How can I tell you how sexy you are in that ankle-length pale blue dress as you flow through the screen of my mind, flashing "PRESS ANY BUTTON"? What can I say but I am a coward and would be your angel, your salvation, your slave? If I could just touch the pale skin of your neck, the rosy perfection of your cheek . . . but you are of another world.

The Mennonite girls pass beyond his sight, the skateboarders head off in the opposite direction, no one has come to pick up the rotund Cree family by the back doors, and there is no sign of Raef. How long has Gabe been lost in thought, unable to speak? He isn't sure . . . they've missed the 9:30, he knows that much, but the sun still hasn't set, he sees it reflected in the cold glass windows of the high-rise condos. The light hurts his eyes. The thought of starting all over in Vancouver, where they can never have too many drug counsellors (not that he actually has anything lined up), of delivering the brand new 80-thousand-dollar Mercedes to his smug brother-in-law, having to learn about sea-buses and sky-trains, of having nothing but what could be put in two suitcases and an old army footlocker . . . the whole thing makes the earth stop spinning, roots his feet to the ground.

He doesn't sense Raef's reappearance; he is too lost in his dismal reverie to catch the tiny, ironic smile that slithers to the corners of his friend's mouth.

"I don't know who the ghost was," Raef begins, "me or the security guys. It was amazing; they didn't seem to hear a word I was saying. I'd say, 'Hanger, you know, to unlock the car, phone, to call a tow truck . . . *comprende?*'"

"I was thinking the same thing," Gabe says distantly. "I mean, we go from your place to the car, to the shopping mall and hang out in the middle of the street . . . and it's like we never left your living room. I have the same feeling at home. Sometimes I even go to the corner store in my pajamas. It's right downstairs, three doors over. I don't think about it, I just throw a coat over my pee-jays and off I go. There are other people around, sure, but the feeling is the same. We smoke our little joints out in the world but we are completely self-contained, only mobile. The screen just changes. I've been watching that fat family not getting picked up, waiting for nothing, the little girls . . . I wasn't actually going to talk to them, touch them . . . even in Friendly Manitoba, what would be the point? We don't exist for them. You're right, ghosts. We may as well still be in your living room hiding from the sun, pressing any fucking button and getting it over with."

The last glint of sunlight bounces from the gleaming ultra-white hood of Arielle's brand new Cabriolet convertible directly into their eyes. She pulls up beside Gabe and Raef, dangling a set of car keys.

"Good thing you remembered I have your spares, I had totally forgotten," she says. "Luckily I was on my way out . . ."

The glow is not coming from the sun anymore, but from Arielle. She is several months pregnant and wears a stranger's ring on her finger. Her face flushes with joy as she recognizes Gabriel.

"Oh my God, how long has it been?" she exclaims. "We should get some people together, have a thing . . . how long are you going to be around?"

"I have to leave first thing in the morning," Gabe answers, and has no idea why.

JUST BOB

*T*here really is no reason to write about Bob.

Like most people, Bob's got a story. He's got two ex-wives he hasn't seen in years. He's also got a kid from each of them; a boy and a girl now both in their 20s. He sees them all the time. Hell, he even has a grandson. Bob works sometimes, landscaping, house painting . . . he collects UI when he can, welfare when he can't. He was the assistant handyman for an old guy who owned some buildings in the neighbourhood for almost nine years . . . that was back when he still had to pay child support.

Now he's got a dog and a lady friend who comes around a couple of times a week. He watches sports on TV. He's always in for a little softball in the summer, video golf on his PlayStation all year round. Some other games too, mostly sports and combat.

That's the basic story.

Not much, or just enough, or maybe it's what you make of it, as lives go, but as for stories . . . well, everybody's got 'em. We've all seen some weird shit, even Bob, even this Bob, who is just Bob. There are other Bobs, of course, more interesting sounding Bobs, too. I've met a Guatemalan Bob, English Bob, Gypsy Bob, Bob Next-door, Downtown Bob, Little Bob, Big Bob and even a Humungo Bob. I'm not going to go into all the Bobbys because this Bob is not a Bobby. No one calls him Bobby. Not his long dead mother, either of his ex-wives, none of his buddies, most of whom he's known since high school . . . no one.

This Bob is just Bob.

If you want his stories, they can't be found in his name.

To his credit, Bob is the sort of guy, once you've got a couple of beers into him, who will whet the air with a clack of tongue on upper palate followed by the dreaded, "I could tell you stories, boy . . ." then he laughs, just long enough for someone to cut him off. Bob offers you the choice between being fish or fisherman, bite his hook or send out your lure.

As stories go . . . well, it all depends on your criteria and the story on the floor that has to be topped. I had a dog who was so smart, a kid who was so vicious, a buddy who was so tough, we all drank so much that . . . You've heard it all before. Who hasn't? Perhaps Bob's stories have some clever twist, a new angle, at least a couple of good descriptive passages for the action lovers in the crowd. The question is: can you bear to hear them out, or are you too busy preparing your response? You have to be ready to top the topper, be the alpha, own the room, because storytelling is a highly competitive business.

Before you get involved, you have to ask yourself if Bob is really worth the investment. Moreover, can one derive the essence of Bob without knowing the particulars?

Starting from the outside, one notes that Bob is a mid-sized man, in good shape, possibly still in his 40s, but not. When he unleashes his broad, toothy smile, you can see the fine wrinkles about his medium-brown eyes. He's had the same boyish haircut since he was a boy. He bears no signs of balding, but definitely has some grey creeping in on the fringes. He has rough hands with yellowed nails. Bob has a faded green smudge tattoo on his right bicep . . . I'm sure it meant something once.

All this doesn't tell us very much.

The problem is, sorting through Bob's stories won't necessarily paint a truer portrait. We may learn at what point he resorts to violence, or did when he was a younger, more volatile man, how he trained his children and fed his dog. Maybe he'll provide some home improvement tips from his handyman days, an opinion on sports which tells you how he plays the game, or, if there're only guys in the room, maybe he'll share something a little down and dirty. Regardless, there remains the dilemma of the persona Bob projects when telling a story. How can we know how close Performing Bob is to Real Bob?

Let's just sit back and watch him, make a study of mannerism and reaction, blend into the habitat, sit down for Chrissake and have a drink.

Bob's got a pretty loud laugh and a tendency to knee slap, you'll notice that right off the bat. He seems to have no problem making himself comfortable either, even on these awkward wood tavern chairs. I hate them. They're the kind with the round arms that come all the way from the back, and inevitably leave splinters in my ass. Bob's jacket, a pale-blue windbreaker, doesn't fall to the floor. Bob is able to recline. It seems so easy for him, leaning back, kicking one foot out under the table and curling the other into the leg of the chair.

The waitress brings him a draft without asking, runs a tab based on a look, barely avoids getting her ass slapped by one of Bob's buddies, and heads harrumphing back to the bar. Bob laughs at his buddy's antics, but it's not his usual laugh. It seems forced . . . the waitress might know. She knows to bring him a draft; she knows his shtick and the quality of men he associates with. Maybe she should be writing about Bob. Maybe she is.

More people come in and they all seem to know Bob. A small crowd gathers. Tables are pushed together. Chairs are rearranged. The rabble settle back in. Rounds of drinks are ordered and distributed. Smokes are bummed, lit and shared. One of the other bozos starts going on about something he'd been discussing earlier, something it seems he discusses often. Bob's brow crinkles as he listens, trying to catch up.

Is Bob really listening, or is he preparing his response?

Granted, we all do both at the same time to some extent, but you can see the transition play across Bob's face as his need to respond begins to predominate. First, he breaks eye contact with the speaker, looks up and to the right, as if searching for something in the corner of his brain and then . . . and then he takes in a big breath and the side of him that had been listening is fully subsumed.

"That's a crock of shit and you know it. It's a crock of shit every time you say it!" Bob slams his open hand down on the table. His nostrils flare. A couple of his buddies move in to cool him off. The women usher the bozo into the street and the evening loses its cement. Eventually the bar tabs come to outweigh the resources available. What's left of the crowd is swaying in their seats to late '80s rock ballads. No one is playing pool anymore. Bob settles up as best as he can. Tables and chairs get dragged back to their usual places. The waitress counts her tips.

I go home and continue to not write about Bob.

GOOD JOHN

Margaret lay back into her wall of pillows feeling like a queen. She took a long drag off of her joint. It was good. It was all good. The telephone rang. Let it ring, exhale through the noise, enjoy the peace. The machine picked up on the third ring.

"I'm sorry I can't cum on the phone right now . . ." said Margaret's sexy voice, the low-pitched pro voice . . . throatier than her regular voice, but not by much, not anymore.

"At the sound of the tone (heavy breath) you know what to do."

She turned the volume down.

Where did he get this hash? Where did this guy come from? She knew where he came from. Knew where he lived even. He'd shown her his driver's licence. Who the hell does that? And that smile. It was good, it was always good with him . . . he had these hands. Workman hands, long and strong but somehow . . . soft? Not soft, supple. Supple. She stubbed the joint out. What was she thinking? She was thinking of calling him later. He'd given her his phone number. She knew it was the real one too. She'd looked it up. He'd said she could call if she was in trouble . . . what if she just wanted to talk? That was serious trouble.

The phone rang again.

The machine picked up. Margaret's throatier recorded voice answered in whispers.

The first time with him she knew it was something different. He'd hung out afterwards, hadn't bothered to get dressed, just went to the bathroom naked and came right back to bed. Usually they can't wait to get their clothes back on and get the hell out, either that or they're hoping for seconds on the house. They'd watched TV naked, smoked this kick-ass hash he says he always has. When she'd leaned into him, nestling her head into the crook of his arm, he hadn't tensed. He had accepted her. Welcomed her. Ran his fingers through her hair. It felt brittle, she could hear it cracking, but he didn't say a thing.

She'd told him her name.

She relit the joint and glanced at her answering machine. Neither caller had left a message.

They never do. That was three weeks ago.

•   •   •

April gets off the bus one stop early. It's not that she needs the exercise, she's already had her morning run, taught four straight phys. ed. classes, run the after-school gymnastics practice and done her after-work work-out. She just wants to see the building again. She wants to remind herself of . . . Margaret? Herself? No, it was her other self, May. It was May who took money for sex, not April. It was May, not April who was only doing it to "pay her way through grad school." That's what May/April told any of them who bothered to ask.

April checks her watch and starts her run.

It was that phone call a couple of weeks ago, Margaret out of the blue. Margaret calling her at work. Margaret even knowing her number at work . . . at first, that old pro talking was like one of April's lust-struck, starry-eyed eighth graders, a mile a minute with no punctuation and no time to breathe. Margaret breaking Margaret's number three rule for survival in the life: Don't give them your name.

Why was she surprised? Margaret still hadn't followed the number two rule: Get out before it gets you. April had. Two years at Gentleman's Choice Escorts to pay for grad school, another five months with Top-Flight Girls Inc. to build up a little nest egg and out like a thief in the night, free as a bird without a cent in student loans to pay back. It was all so easy except . . . except she never would have gotten through that first week without Margaret.

Margaret wasn't running Gentleman's Choice when April went to work there, but she wasn't just one of the girls either. Sometimes she answered the phone. Sometimes she took a call. Now, Margaret is an old whore out on her own. A whore in her own home. Still, it was Margaret's shoulder April had cried on after May's third trick.

"It's usually the third one that breaks the tough ones," Margaret had said. "And you're about the toughest little number I've ever seen." April had laughed at that, had felt comforted by the smell of Margaret's perfume, her soft flesh . . . everything was alright after that. April hasn't cried since. She hasn't laughed much either.

She rounds the corner and looks up at the house where she'd first met Margaret. Why'd she gotten off the bus back there? She could see the house from her own 34th-floor concrete box of an apartment three blocks away.

"He's honest," Margaret had said. So what?

April looks at her watch. Quarter to eight. She can get in a two-mile run and still be home in time for *Survivor*.

She turns from the house and runs away from where she lives.

• • •

Tracy made sure everyone's mother was there to pick them up before going to the locker room. She let all the other girls take their showers first. She brushed her teeth thoroughly, flossed, peed twice, talked to Melanie about her stupid birthday party for like an hour (five minutes), and dawdled any other way she could think of to make sure she would be the last girl out of the room.

She smiles her secret smile as she slowly re-laces her boots. That ought to give them enough time, she thinks. She wishes there were a spy-hole somewhere in the locker room so she can watch them. Maybe she should be there, you know, to help. She wasn't pleased with the way things went the last time. Maybe she should have been there the last time. Well, she sort of was. Maybe that was the problem. She'd only given them a couple of minutes together, she had been too impatient to wait it out.

"So what do you think of Ms. Hudson, Daddy? Isn't she pretty?" Tracy had managed to wait until they were high up in the cab of Daddy's truck before asking.

"I guess so," he said in a way Tracy didn't like one little bit.

Daddy saw that right away, he always did.

"To be honest, sweetheart, I don't think she likes me very much." He put his hand on her leg. "She looked at me in a way . . . I just know that look. The LOOK."

He did, too. Daddy always knows what people are feeling, that's what makes him so special. Why couldn't Ms. Hudson see that? Tracy didn't understand why everybody didn't fall in love with Daddy at first sight. She didn't get Daddy either. He was like the most handsome man *ever*. Didn't he know that? He should be out there dating supermodels or something, but the only woman Tracy has ever seen him with was that crazy drug-bitch who came to the house that time. It's not like he kissed her or anything, he just gave her some money and explained to Tracy later that she was an old friend who was down on her luck. Tracy wanted to believe him, but she also wanted to believe he had some kind of romantic life. It's not that she wanted a new mommy or anything, although it would be really cool if Ms. Hudson became her stepmother, it's just that Daddy deserves something, someone . . .

Tracy heard things sometimes when Daddy talked on his phone or listened to his messages, but that crazy (down-on-her-luck, my ass) crack-ho was as close as Tracy had come to actually seeing Daddy with anyone.

"I offered to help her put some of the equipment away, but she didn't want *my help,* she said. The important thing is she seems to care about you and she does her job well, right? She is a good gymnastics coach, right?"

"She's the best!"

"Are you hungry, sweetheart? Do you want to go out for dinner?"

"She's so smart, too . . ."

"We'll go anywhere you like . . ."

"Daddy, are you listening to me?"

"I'm hanging on every word," and he smiled. "Now, we'll go eat whatever you like . . . is it pizza?"

"How did you know?"

He always knew.

• • •

Margaret curls into her blankets and tries to remember the first time she'd actually pulled together enough courage to give him a call. She'd tortured herself all day. Picking up the phone, dialling five or six digits and then hanging up. Right to the edge but never over. When she finally punched in the last digit, her eyes were closed and her head was turned away from the phone.

"Is it a bad time to call? I got your message earlier . . ."

"Not at all. Perfect timing, really." His voice sounded so warm on the phone.

"I had fun the other day . . ."

She shouldn't have said that. Margaret cringes in her blanket cocoon as the memory of her little-girl skittishness floods her body, mind and soul.

"Me too," he'd said, like a shy seven-year-old.

They'd laughed.

Margaret relaxes her grip on her pillow and smiles. He was such a funny guy in just the way she likes.

"How come a guy like you doesn't have a girlfriend?" she'd finally asked.

"I don't believe in them."

"You never fall in love?"

"Love is impossible in a transactional society."

"You're full of shit."

"Everyone is."

"I think you're a nice guy."

"Thank you. I think you're a nice woman." His tone had become suddenly serious, intense. Margaret kicked herself for letting it go, reverting to funny to escape what could have been . . .

"You're so full of shit," she'd shot back at him. "What I mean is that you're not the Iceman you pretend to be."

"Everyone is what they pretend to be . . . until someone else breaks through the pretense."

"A fucking philosopher."

"A dreamer and a realist."

"A joker, a smoker, a midnight toker?"

"I get my lovin' on the run."

"C'mon over, Steve Miller. Shake my tree."

"Call me John."

"I call 'em all John. The thing is I want to . . . jeez, this is hard . . ."

"I can't swing by today. Maybe tomorrow. No, tomorrow for sure."

"Business?"

"Family. I'm glad you called."

The way he'd said that word. Family. Margaret replayed it again and again in her mind. It blocked out the other, darker thoughts that had been waiting to pounce. Why would a guy that good-looking, that young, that charming, want to be with her?

Family. His voice. That word. She could feel it growing in her like an addiction.

·   ·   ·

April decides not to cut through the park, but to go around it. She needed the run to cool off. Who was she pissed at? Margaret? Herself? Or that guy — Tracy's father? Coming in when the girls were in the shower. Coming into her gym when she was alone, storing the equipment. Something about him . . . the way their eyes met.

"Can I give you a hand?"

Was she attracted to him? Was that the problem? Was that even possible? That was the first time he intruded. Then there's what happened today . . .

She's angry with Margaret, too. Margaret, coming back into her life, reminding her of things best left forgotten. Margaret, who called the school again today, even after April had told her in no uncertain terms the last time that she shouldn't call her at work. What does she want? What can April really do for her?

As she rounds the corner, April sees a madwoman. Angry and crazy. She is pacing between the door of the St. James methadone clinic and the pay phone on the corner, kicking at cracks in the sidewalk, muttering a long stream of profanities. April jogs in place, waiting for the light to change. The madwoman picks up the phone, slams it down and starts her march back to the door of the clinic.

April decides to go past the park and circle back by the river. What the hell, so she'd miss the first half of *Survivor*. They don't kick anyone off the show until the end.

April takes off at her six-minute-mile pace.

• • •

Stupid Jeanine said she forgot her stupid retainer in her stupid locker and had to come back to the locker room for it. Tracy didn't believe her. She knew the truth. Jeanine's cow-faced mother likes Daddy and sent Jeanine in here so she could corner him. What a disaster. Now he'd never be alone with Ms. Hudson. Didn't ugly Jeanine's ugly mother know that Daddy didn't like her? How could he? Ms. Hudson was the one for him. She was perfect, smart and cool and so pretty. Tracy hoped her body would look like that when she grew up, even if it's "a little too long and curvy for a competitive gymnast."

All the work Tracy had done over the past three weeks — finding out that Ms. Hudson doesn't have a boyfriend, isn't a lesbian, doesn't have AIDS, use drugs, drink or own a car. Tracy had given Daddy her full report over breakfast, pointing out that this was the last practice of the season and he should really make a move.

"I already have a girlfriend," he'd said.

"No you don't!"

"Sure I do. I got you." He kissed her forehead, cupping the base of her neck with his long fingered hands in that way he had that made her melt. Maybe he should just put his hand through Ms. Hudson's hair that way, maybe that's all it would take.

"My mother's waiting in the car, so I gotta go. Bye!" cheery Jeanine says, stuffing her retainer into her mouth.

• • •

April runs past Margaret's building then cuts back. She half decides to go upstairs to . . . confront Margaret? Hug her? Let her break down and have a good old-fashioned cry? Is that what Margaret wants? Doesn't she owe Margaret at least that much? Her hard shoulder to cry on?

"I don't charge him," Margaret had said.

Instead, they had a fair trade agreement. He had been helping her remodel her apartment. "He used to do construction work, but now he owns the company. He still dives a pickup, though. That's so sexy, don't you think? He said he misses the 'hands on'. I get so turned on watching him work. He's got these long muscles, you know?"

An image of Tracy's father flashes in April's mind. He had these long taut forearms . . . delicate fingers. He had this calculated smile and open eyes. She pictures him shirtless, up in the cab of his midnight-blue monster truck, the window down, the wind in his hair . . .

"He fucks like a porno star. I swear to God. When I think about it afterwards, which is unbelievable to begin with, I see it like a dirty movie in my head," Margaret had laughed. "There he is, tiling my bathroom and I just jump him. It was fantastic. You have any idea what it's like to get it when *you* want it?"

"Do you like my Daddy?" Tracy had asked.

April couldn't answer.

She stares up at Margaret's window, jogging in place, taking her pulse. One-forty-four. Maybe he was up there, Margaret's Good John, fixing her plumbing but good!

"I told him I loved him."

Margaret had broken her number one rule.

April had heard the panic in the background of her voice, even then, three weeks ago. She can only imagine what Margaret had sounded like on the phone this morning. "Troubled," the secretary who'd taken the message had said.

April is overwhelmed with resentment towards Margaret for making her feel like she owes her something, for making her feel some kind of connection to the past that she thought she'd severed, for making her feel . . .

April turns on her heels and picks up her pace.

• • •

Margaret pulls her two extra pillows under the covers and curls into them. It's been ten days since he said he'd call back. Ten days of withdrawal. Eight days of staring at the call-display screen on her phone through tears. Six days since she'd stopped taking tricks and three hours since she last tried to call him. She got his machine again and couldn't push any words from her throat. She'd breathed heavily and hung up.

The phone rings. If it's him, he'll leave a message. If it's him, she'll know by the sound of the ring. She had been almost sure at seven, but had been wrong. It was "Sonny." She vaguely remembers him. She recognized his number on the display. He has an ugly bald-ape head and deformed little ears. She isn't up to it. Not up to any john but John.

Margaret uncurls from her pillows and sits up. She reaches for the ashtray she'd tipped onto the floor two days ago. She hadn't bothered to pick it up, hadn't had to. She'd been using a small pink plate instead. She empties the plate and then the ashtray into her popcorn bowl and begins sifting for roaches. She must have smoked fifteen joints since . . . since she'd tipped the ashtray. She sees patches of her warped reflection in the dirty pink plate. Her wrinkles, laugh-lines she calls them, deep and comically extended. She doesn't laugh. She picks out five of the juicier roaches and crumbles them onto the cover of *TV Guide*. She snips the end off of her second to last cigarette. Maybe she'd take a client if he picked up some smokes. She breaks the clipped cigarette in half.

"Shit."

The telephone rings. It isn't him. She can feel it. Maybe it's April calling back. Or, more likely some prospective john, so maybe she should pick up, if only to get him to grab her some smokes on his way over. The caller registers as "private number." The machine picks up. The caller disconnects. Margaret's tear-wet fingertips weaken her rolling paper. She rips her joint in two.

"Fucking-shit-mother-fucker!"

She throws the TV guide across the room.

The telephone rings again. Maybe she should just pull her ad out of the paper.

Margaret throws herself into her wall of pillows. The answering machine picks up.

The caller hangs up.

• • •

Sylvia slams the receiver down and wrenches her quarter from the slot.

The fucking clinic closes in ten fucking minutes and he won't fucking pick up. Screening his fucking calls. You gotta love the prick. What the fuck did he care anyways? He came the closest, give him that much. He was fine until . . . until she fell for him. That was the death of it. That was the death of it every time. "Man's Disease," they should call it. Symptoms: when told he is loved, the patient will flee.

Her "Good John," she'd called him, until he wasn't. He had these long hands . . . but that was months ago. He had to have a new whore by now. What did he care? Sylvia did have to admit to herself that she never should have gone up to his place that time, but she was out of her fucking mind then, he had to know that. She was better now, or would be if she could get her fucking meth . . . If not, fucking anything could happen. He knew that.

Here comes little Miss Fitness again. Jesus, she's looking right the fuck at me. Who the fuck does she think she is? What a fucking body though.

"Excuse me."

Fucking ignoring me or what?

"Yeah, Miss, I'm talking to you. Do I know you? Then why are you looking at me?"

"I saw you here before. Are you alright?"

"No, I'm not fucking alright. I'm on the program and the fuckers in there won't let me get my stuff unless I give them the forty fucking bucks I don't fucking have."

Sylvia spits on the window of the clinic. She spits on April's cross-trainers. She snarls. April stares at her.

Cold.

• • •

Tracy wants to know everything. When she'd come out of the locker room they'd been there, just the two of them, and they'd been talking, she could tell. There was something in the air — Tracy thought it smelled like sex, but she couldn't be sure. She didn't know what sex smelled like. Ms. Hudson had a look on her face Tracy had never seen before. Was she in love with Daddy? Did it work? She was dying to know but Daddy wasn't saying anything.

"Hang on, honey. Daddy's got to check his messages. He's expecting an important business call."

Tracy hated it when he talked business on his cellphone when they were in the truck together. He was supposed to be talking to her, instead he was all "scratching each other's backs and as long as we're better-looking, they're the trick."

He's got his phone pinned between his shoulder and ear and he's smiling at her.

"What did you say to Ms. Hudson . . . ?"

"Just a sec," he says

"Hon, it's me, Sylvia. I'm at my clinic, but I don't have the scratchola to get what I need, it's like quarter to . . . I'm at the phone booth . . ." Tracy can hear the crack-witch's voice before Daddy forwards over the rest of the message. Why is she calling now? Is she trying to ruin everything?

"Hon, I don't want to bother you, but . . ." Her again!

"It's me, Syl . . ."

The fourth caller breathed heavily and hung up. Tracy didn't know who that one was, but Daddy did. He smiled when he heard it.

"So what do you want tonight, sweetheart . . . Chinese?"

"I want to know what happened with you and Ms. Hudson."

"So you don't want Chinese?"

"Dad-dy!"

"I think I'd like to see April again," he says. "Maybe I'll give her a call."

Tracy knew it! Daddy got her number!

• • •

Margaret knew that she should have known . . . not that it helped much. What did he want with her in the first place? She'd been advertising herself as, "Mature woman, 43 . . ." for at least five years. He couldn't be much past 35. He was handsome, successful, dressed business-casual better than anyone she'd met . . . what did he want? What kind of sick fetishist is this guy? Why won't he at least come over here and let me tell him off, suck his dick . . . whatever.

Margaret also had to admit that she missed his dope. He comes along, shows her she still has a heart so he could stomp all over it and doesn't even have the fucking courtesy to leave her enough medicine to get over it. Maybe he just needed some distance. The whole thing had snow-balled so quickly. We slept together on the first date, Margaret thinks. She nearly smiles. She wasn't his girlfriend. She really didn't have the right to expect anything.

More importantly, she had to get ready for Sonny. Maybe he had something? She doubted it. He often smelled of booze but never brought any. Margaret shudders as she undresses. The water spewing from her shower is lukewarm at best. It will probably be just plain cold when she'll be washing Sonny off of her in an hour or so. He'd better remember the cigarettes.

Margaret notices the hair in the drain. Her hair. Brittle from years of Miss Clairol even when it's wet.

He'll be back.

Margaret feels tears roll down her face. They're warmer than the water.

You just have to laugh.

She does.

• • •

Sylvia loses her balance and staggers forward towards April. She catches the toe of her boot in the sidewalk and her stagger turns into a lunge. April sidesteps the falling Sylvia, spins and delivers a roundhouse kick to her ribs. Sylvia careens off the pay phone and hits the ground face first. April thinks she hears something shatter, but the pay phone seems undamaged. Sylvia raises her fist and it flails at April. April delivers two precision kicks to Sylvia's head.

April is about to deliver another shot when she realizes it isn't the madwoman she's kicking. Not in her heart. It's him. Tracy's father. Right there in the gym. Today. His eyes boring into her. His long arms first folded over his chest then extending out, the long fingers uncurling.

"How much?"

"Excuse me?"

"Don't bullshit me. You know what I'm talking about. I can see it in your eyes. You think you're hiding it, but I can see it."

"What do you want?"

"Not what you think, well not only . . ."

"I think this is very inappropriate . . ."

"Jesus Christ, you have the coldest heart I've ever seen."

"Seen?"

"I can see it and I want it. I want to melt it in my hands."

April stared at his long beautiful fingers, she was flushed and paralyzed, he kept looking at her right in the eyes . . . she wanted to say something, to scream, to kick . . .

Then Tracy came out of the locker room and ran to her Daddy, wrapping her arms around his waist, feeling his taut torso, his hands running through her hair.

April looks down. Sylvia is sobbing into the sidewalk.

"There's this guy I used to know. I thought he might help, but he isn't home and if I don't get . . . then I don't know what the fuck I'm going to do, because and that smug piece of shit in there . . ."

Sylvia doesn't even feel the hole in her chest caused by April's first kick. She feels only a warm, sticky wave expanding across her body, centred at the point where April's foot had driven the needle from her shattered fix.

April turns from the dying madwoman, resets her stopwatch and heads out at her six-minute-mile pace.

A Master of the Fecal Arts

*D*ylan could have let the voice mail pick up. He knew who it was. The world had come into focus quickly enough for him to read "DAD" on the tiny green screen of his cellphone. He was faced with the all too common dilemma of being furious with his father and the incessantly ringing telephone — god, how he hated that stupid little cellphone — and realizing it was well past noon and there was no need to give the old man the satisfaction of catching him sleeping in. Not that Dylan's father would voice any objection. He wasn't like that. He'd quietly note it, allow it to become just another in a series of incidents used in the formation of "a pattern of behavior."

Alert enough to read the screen means alert enough to answer, to pretend to be busy . . . though he doubted his father would see prancing about his small, windowless studio buck-naked looking for a roll of toilet paper as indicative of work getting done . . . Dylan has to settle for a small stack of napkins from Wendy's. Seeing her shit-smeared smiling little red-headed face will have to make up for the lack of comfort.

"Am I calling at a bad time?" His father starts every conversation this way. It's an excellent means of "establishing parameters."

"Not at all, I was just finishing my lunch and getting ready to get back to work," Dylan said, sucking the melted ice water from the Biggie Diet Coke that had come with his Double Bacon Cheese Big Classic Combo the previous night. "Maybe I'll go to the bathroom first. Who knows?"

"How's your work coming?"

"Fine," Dylan responded brightly, thinking, leave it to the old man to make the segue from going to the bathroom to my art. "In fact, never better. I'm waiting for some materials to come in for a project I've had in mind for some time. It's on a much larger scale than I've ever attempted. In the meantime I'm doing some sketches."

"Interesting . . ."

"I can show you some of them, if you like."

"If you feel they're ready for viewing . . ."

Dylan didn't like the tone in the old man's voice, he wasn't taking the bait. "I'll be working with wood again, I'm thinking of taking a course in cabinetmaking, to get the feel for it again . . ."

"It's a noble trade."

Dylan knew what that meant. Not only was the old man in no mood to cough up some coin, he was going to have his say, inasmuch as he ever said anything. "It's a noble trade" really means go back to university and take those two courses for your Teaching Certificate. It really means give up being an artist, have a default position at least (same thing), grow up, for crying out loud . . . and it meant none of it. His father would never discourage Dylan's art . . . he may occasionally present possible scenarios, point out that earning a decent wage isn't a crime. Even if they were actually having the conversation they were really having, Dylan's father would still just claim to be giving pragmatic suggestions, playing devil's advocate, by no means trying to dictate the terms of Dylan's life.

Dylan, still naked after giving his clothes a quick sniff, darted out of his studio. He ran past the space shared by Lou-Ellen and that conceptual artist guy from Slovakia, his bare feet getting progressively numb from the January air wafting in from somewhere. The previous night's indulgences churned in his gut while he kept up with his father's passive third degree.

"Are you sure you have enough space in your studio?"

"Do you want to come over and measure?"

Dylan bounded up the stairs to the big loft on the top floor. The room had been painted the previous day making the walls so white they glowed, unlike Dylan's very brown, crumbling rathole downstairs, which hadn't seen a drop of paint or smidgen of spackle since the age of the horse-drawn cart. The painters had left all the windows open, which accounted for the ungodly cold that tore into Dylan's naked flesh. The toilet, a very small, very stained model with no seat or cover, sat on a small wooden alter. A thin layer of ice had begun to take form in the bowl.

"I'm sorry, I was momentarily distracted by an interesting ice configuration."

That line set the old man off. Dylan had to know it would.

"I was just asking your sister if she still had that photograph you took of the river in Moron Heights. Do you remember the one I mean?"

Dylan grunted his assent. He was again of two minds: bitter that the old man had slipped off the hook, and relieved that he could concentrate on the business at hand — trying to excrete the half-pound of red meat he'd engorged the night before. He only half listened to his father's comparative experiential analysis of the aesthetics of ice. Dylan's father had taken several photographs of ice back in the 70s. He was no Ansel Adams and perhaps he didn't have Dylan's natural eye but . . .

Dylan rarely ate red meat, he rarely ate anything but cornflakes with bananas, but he'd gotten together with some old friends from high school, a bunch of suburban conformist morons . . . they were alright, he guessed. They bought the drinks, paid for the burgers. Jamie even treated him to some blow before dropping him off at the studio. He couldn't go to Monica's drunk and wired. That was rule number one, and since he was temporarily between apartments of his own . . . The old man was really *en forme*, dredging up memories of photographs in some back issue of *The Smithsonian* he'd always been keen on. Dylan had heard it all before. He intoned at the appropriate junctures and wondered for the millionth time if the old man was for real.

Doesn't he realize that not everything comes down to a series of examples leading to a pattern? Does he really have to go through this prolonged and terrible process to come to the inevitable conclusion that ice can be beautiful? Just say it! Ice is beautiful. Just feel it. Just express it. Of course, that's exactly what the old man's doing . . . in the only way he knows.

Given the ambient temperature and the lack of a seat, Dylan had to squat inches above the toilet seat with his cellphone in one hand and the Wendy's napkins in the other, making his balance somewhat precarious.

"Are you taking up ice sculpture?"

"No, just noticing a pattern." Dylan realized that, despite his best efforts, he was being reintegrated into the conversation, actual words would have to flow forth.

"You did that once, didn't you?"

"In summer camp."

"That's right. I forget how that went . . ."

"Not very well. It's more of a winter activity, really . . ." The words trailed off and the beef would not pass. Trust the old man to bring up past triumphs. What lies at the centre of a passive aggressive? Is there anything? Who's Dylan to talk? The great artist? The great bullshit artist, maybe. Monica's bound to figure it out pretty soon. He could only lie about sleeping with Lou-Ellen for so long, get away with pinching cash from her purse so often, and since he had no intention of stopping either practice anytime soon . . . but the old man just won't come out and say it.

"Look," Dylan's father said after a short but uncomfortable silence. "I've always said that after your eighteenth birthday you are the state's responsibility, not mine. I'll help any way I can, but it's your life."

That did it.

A sharp, stabbing contraction reverberated through Dylan's abdomen and he could feel jagged bacon bits tearing their way through his sphincter. The sensation was so intensely painful, such an excruciating relief, that despite the nasty northerly wind cutting in from the open windows, despite seeing his father's half-concerned, half-sardonic face clear as finest crystal in his mind's eye, he had an erection.

"That's alright. I'm fine. Mom said she'd pay for half of the materials I ordered. I can pay for the other half if I have to," he said after another ugly pause.

"If I'm calling at a bad time . . ."

"Not at all, couldn't be better. My battery is fully charged."

"Unlike when I usually call."

"I'm sorry about that. I actually remembered to plug the stupid phone in when I got to the studio. Are you busy?"

What a colossal blunder. "Are you busy?" The old man has only one answer for that one.

He went on to describe in minute detail his entire agenda for the following week. He had a meeting with the Society of Civil Engineers on Monday morning, then lunch with Jack Middleton, back to the office until five, pick up the evening paper and the dry cleaning on the way home . . .

Dylan, still fairly weak in the knees, tried to stand up. When he was about 80 percent up he had a major head rush and nearly lost his footing altogether. He fanned his arms out for balance, took a deep breath and sighed it out . . . Tuesday night his father was going to a movie with Dylan's older sister. Dylan was welcome to come along and Monica too . . . Dylan placed his cellphone on top of the stack of Wendy's napkins in his left hand. He then pulled two of the napkins from the bottom, swung his head to the other side, smiled at the slickness of his move and wiped his ass. Still smiling, he'd need the rest of the napkins later, his bowels were being pretty clear on that point, Dylan folded one of the napkins semi-inside-out with one hand and wiped again.

Ah, the artistry.

Dylan looked down to see his morning erection still in full bloom. Amazing. Maybe he should tell his father about it, if only to get away from hearing the rest of his weekly agenda. The old man would start talking about the frequency of his own morning erections, probably not so many anymore, although you never know.

Dylan's father was to play squash with Douglas Reid before Friday night dinner at Aunt Ruth's. Dylan was in for that one. He couldn't say no to Ruth's cooking, even if he couldn't imagine ever eating again. Maybe he could hit the old man up at Ruth's. If that was the plan, then the movie was definitely out. He looked down to admire his erect penis again, and that's when it happened.

Dylan, ever so lightly, loosened his grip on his cellphone. The hated contraption slipped from its perch on the remaining Wendy's napkins in his right hand, bounced first off his chest then his left thigh. As it hung suspended in mid-air for the longest fraction of a second, Dylan made a swipe for it with his right hand, managing to keep it in the air and sending the remaining napkins fluttering yellow to the floor. Then his left hand got into the action, bouncing the phone off the inside of his right shoulder, where again it seemed to stop for the most fleeting of moments before rolling down his arm, through his grasping fingers and directly into the rust-stained, unflushed bowl.

Dylan let out a short scream, flinched his eyes shut, twisted his body hard to the left and plunged his hand into the steaming hot and utter cold of the toilet. His panicked fingers thrashed madly until they found and wrapped themselves around the small plastic body. The little screen came up black, the keypad unlit. Dylan sniffed the phone then jerked out his arm, almost losing it again. He took a deep breath and, holding the phone at arm's length, bent down to pick up the napkins. He wrapped the phone in one of them, placed it between his feet for safekeeping while he wiped his hands with the other two.

Dylan dejectedly picked up his phone again and made his way to the door. Door? He hadn't noticed a door at the top of the stairs leading into the loft, but there it was, big, made of steel and firmly locked. He gave the big steel door three futile punches, let out a couple of feeble cries for help and sunk to the floor. Well, this is it. The great tragic end . . . He looked at the cellphone in his hand. Maybe, just maybe . . . He pressed the power button and the little green light shone like a beacon. The awful sharp tone that indicates someone has left a message echoed through the frozen loft. Dylan hit his quick key for voice mail and tried to remember Lou-Ellen's phone number.

The message was from his father. Dylan only got to listen to the first few words, "What happened? Did you drop your phone in the—" before, as miraculously as it had just come on, the phone died again.

Somewhere from deep within Dylan, from a place that's deeper and usually more silent than the incessant suicidal nagging his mind likes to conjure, more compelling than the morose whine telling him he should have masturbated when he had the chance — it may have been his last, stronger in essence than his well-proven instinct for self-destruction — came a tremendous burst of laughter. He tried to contain it. He flexed his muscles and turned down his mouth, but it rose like a tidal wave in him. He started trembling and coughing out giggles, then to shake and roll on the ground. The giggle turned into a cackle. He cackled until he hiccupped. His arms slapped the floor uncontrollably. Unable to properly breathe, his laughter came out like a hysterical sheep bleating.

Then he was still.

Almost. He stopped shaking from the laughter and began shivering from the cold.

Suicide via submission to the cold having been ruled out by the hysterical fit, Dylan snapped into action.

He closed the windows and tried to turn on the baseboard heater, which yielded a promising but eventually disappointing bang and sputter from somewhere below. He found the stack of drop cloths the painters had left in the far corner of the room and wrapped himself in them as tightly as he could. Eventually his teeth were no longer chattering, his legs and arms came under control, his focus clear. The old man would be proud, Dylan thought. Here I am being pragmatic under pressure.

He removed the battery from the back of his cellphone and placed it on the extended corner of his robe of drop cloths. He took the small plastic-coated chip from the exposed body of the phone and put it beside the battery. He spent the next several minutes meticulously drying the components. He wasn't sure if he should reassemble it immediately or let it wait awhile to make sure it was actually dry. What about ice crystals forming? Even with the windows closed it was well below freezing in the loft.

The loft.

Dylan stopped his fidgeting to admire it. He'd been up here before, but it had been cluttered and subdivided by tall partitions. The last tenants had run some kind of a boiler room. With the partitions down and the fresh paint — what a difference! What a space! Three of the 20-foot-high walls had high arching windows, allowing the whole loft to reverberate with natural light from dawn 'til dusk. Unlike Dylan's windowless little cubbyhole downstairs, this was a place to work in. If he had this space maybe he wouldn't be so blocked. Maybe he'd actually start doing sketches for some big project. Maybe the money his mother had sent him for materials would actually go to purchasing materials, instead of chipping in for groceries and Monica's phone bill and a little dime bag of weed to steady his nerves.

Dylan very gingerly put the phone back together. He took a deep breath and pressed the power button. The green light came on, but his joy was short lived. The dreaded words "INSERT UNIX CHIP" bored their way from the little screen into his heart. He turned the phone off, removed the battery, dried it again and replaced it, making sure the connections met, that the little plastic grooves were properly aligned, and tried again. "INSERT UNIX CHIP"

Dylan took the phone apart, recleaned everything with a fresh corner of drop sheet and was about to try his luck again when he heard an unearthly rumbling. Just as he was beginning to hope that someone was unbolting the door, he realized that his digestive track, the lower part of it at any rate, was responsible for the sound.

Dylan put the phone down and started the knee-crossed fast waddle across the loft to the filthy throne. Two shuffle steps away from the toilet his feet got caught up in one of the drop cloths. He tripped and sprawled, his head coming within a hair's breath of a concussive porcelain blow. His bowels were not offering him the opportunity to remain prostrate.

Using the edge of the toilet bowl for support, Dylan began to raise himself, his hands gripping the edges of the altar.

That's when he saw it.

The dump he had taken earlier and forgotten to flush had frozen into a disk more akin to the dropping of a cow than a man. The leaving was by no means two-dimensional, more oval than round and unlike any cow-puck Dylan had ever seen. Very few cow-pucks look exactly like Dylan's father. The Roman nose, the pronounced forehead, the long thin lips . . . all were perverted into the exact expression Dylan had been picturing, that hated mix of love and sarcasm. He had been picturing it at the exact moment of release! His bowels magically stopped rumbling, the cold ceased to bother him, and he knelt in awe before his creation.

This can't be happening. It's Jamie's fault. That fucking cocaine.

Granted, Jamie was the only one of those "friends" from high school who was still remotely cool. Sure, he had a wife and 2.2 kids and an SUV, but he still knew how to have a good time. He was the only one who'd ever checked out Dylan's studio, had given him a break once in a while. The thing is, it was Jamie's laxative-ridden cocaine that was unravelling Dylan's innards, fucking his mind something fierce.

Yet he opened his eyes again, and there was his father's sardonic face.

Very slowly, Dylan rose to his feet. He unwound from his cloak of paint-splattered tarps and lay them on the floor surrounding the toilet altar, creating a ring of diamonds around his father's mask. Naked again, he raised his arms over his head and took several deep breaths, rising to his toes on the inhale and slumping on the ex. He focused his mind on the image of a solitary pine tree overlooking a lake. There was something familiar about it, not that he'd been there or seen that, his vision was not of the event or object, but the art. When the image finally crystallized, when he was one with it, his body relaxed completely, his heartbeat synchronized with the outpouring from his ass.

He was half afraid to look behind him, but he did.

There on the drop cloth lay Dylan's fecal forgery of his favourite Tom Thomson painting.

The cellphone rang.

Dylan dashed across the room, but was too late, he missed the call. At least the thing was working. He tried to figure out who he should call. His father was out of the question, and there was no way he could face Monica like this. If Lou-Ellen was around she'd have heard him banging on the door. Jamie! What the hell was Jamie's number?

Then a curious thought crossed his mind. Suddenly he wasn't sure if he wanted to be rescued or if he wanted someone to confirm his . . . art.

With the cellphone in his hand he cautiously made his way back to his father and Tom. Were they really there? Had he imagined the whole thing? He had been pretty wired and drunk and stoned. Fuck you, Jamie, and the cold. The cold can twist the mind, or maybe it's the fever. His head burned, his heart raced.

Before he could affirm or deny the forms his feces had taken, or decide who to call, inspiration struck again. He made it to the edge of the second drop cloth and his body buckled. He fell to his hands and knees. His muscles first froze then spasmed violently. A shotgun blast fired from his backside and he crumpled to the floor.

It was several minutes before Dylan could do anything. He knew he couldn't face his father again or the Tom Thomson, if they were really there. Well, he could take another look . . . Then Dylan's eye took in his latest effort.

This one was a self-portrait — Dylan understood that immediately and instinctively. He could see the contours of his being in the hardening mush and knew them for what they were. He smelled his innermost self in the rising, ochre steam.

He knew at once this was his masterpiece, that the others had just been rehearsals. More importantly, he knew it wasn't the end, but only the beginning. In that knowledge is the truth of rebirth, the giving of life that is creation, the life that is art, the art that is my life . . . And inspiration struck again.

This time he didn't even look as he dug his hands into his own clay and began to mould and form. When he needed more materials, out they came. He emptied himself again and again until only a fine yellowish

liquid would grudgingly squirt forth. Dylan gave all he had inside of him
— what else does an artist have to give? Yes, for the first time in his life
he was a real artist, completely free, the inexorable link between vision
and action formed and rooted in Dylan's hollowing gut.

Dylan covered the four canvases about the altar. He moved on to the
floor, sculpting with his hands and feet. He rolled through his creation and
slapped his body against the freshly painted wall. He had no idea whether
he was screaming like a maniac or silent like the dead. Had he banged on
the door for help? Had he screamed out the window, "Come one, come
all!!" Had the terrible cellphone rung or had it died again?

When he finally collapsed in the middle of his creation, spent and
empty, his head resting on the altar, his breath condensing on the under-
side of the stained toilet bowl, Dylan was at peace. He was finally able to
give over, get past the grand deception that is an art career, beyond all the
phony attitudes he'd adopted, the outright lies he'd told Monica, his father
. . . everyone. He smiled and felt genuine love for that half-sardonic, half-
concerned look on his father's face, but he could wait to show it to him.
There was a time when he couldn't . . . Dylan pictured himself calmly listening to his father reminisce about every portrait he's had done — the
school photo in the first grade, the Society of Civil Engineers 25th
anniversary oil on canvas, the family Christmas card from 1987 . . . Dylan
wasn't even growing impatient with the old man, he was joining in,
prompting him: "Oh '87 was good, but what about '79?"

Dylan didn't hear Lou-Ellen and her companion coming up the stairs.
He didn't notice them forcing open the big steel door, he barely felt the
sweater she tried to wrap around his shoulders.

"My god!" Lou-Ellen said. "What a fucking mess."

"What?" said Milan, the conceptual artist from Slovakia. "Is abstract,
yes. Is not too good, yes. But I think is his best work, no?"

THE THEOLLECTUAL CIRCUIT

*I*t is wholly correct to use the word loopy when speaking of the insane. We are referring to their broken-record conversations, the all too human trait of specific obsession we call a falter on the brain. Perhaps the crazy just can't come full circle, from the silence before to the silence after (and they are both and always the silence that underlies), but are caught in a broken version of this inevitable circuit, the rail on which the consciousness rides, that nucleus about which the synapses snap and spark. In an almost tactile way the length and resonance of this bio/spiritual wave is what differentiates you from me, us from them, the crazy from the insane.

In my underlying silence, I spy him through the hinges of his half-open bedroom door. His back is to me. His hands are clasped before him. The light streams in from the rounded window through which he stares.

"What are they looking for?" he asks of the hat-tipping worshippers below. Whether Jew or Gentile, we knew from a casual glance at their cars. He shakes his head. He shrugs his shoulders. He may or may not know I am there . . .

This image of my father, this amalgam of weekend mornings, I've always held warm. It speaks of eventual French toast, of staying in our robes well into the afternoon. It says on this day we may regress back to our beds, in that towering home for the relentlessly self-possessed.

There mounts a genuine desire, a bio-imperative to set the scene; word picture the old Church, the reform Temple, my father's thinning hair, giving time and place . . . context and link . . . but ultimately it is my parents' bedroom, my father's back, the quiver between his shoulder blades and my odd sense of detached complicity that are what is seen.

There is some truth in it after all, Father and Son, Sisterhood, binding relations forming this or that percentage of our combined acknowledged selves, telling the World we are first and foremost *this* and you can call it *that* if you like, but not to my face. This is who I am born and bred to choose to be . . . the whole inevitability of the Mother, the way it all seems so obvious in the fresh Millennium . . .

Yet.

Yet it's nothing new.

I imagine that's what my father saw through the exaggerated clarity of the rounded window. Marx laid it out. Nietzsche exposed it. This Orwellian nightmare insipidly embodied in a brilliantly sunny morning, bearing witness to the faithful returning to their determining cars.

Of course I didn't understand it in those terms back then. Almost, but I wasn't quite past the discarding of that particular veil of ignorance. I like to think I didn't give it any thought back then, give childhood the ol' idyllic twist, the light, that moment, those countless moments of my Father and I unmoved by the hovering dust particles, a ghost in the sunlight between us.

It's really about wondering if there's something in the blood or brain that protects us from these airborne narcofictions. More simply put, what do you do at a pep rally if you don't have genuine pep? You raise your arms with the rest of them and glance furtively about, hoping maybe to connect with another of the disjoined . . . yet dreading it. Fearing there can be no true fraternity of those who do not feel the helping invisible hands, are unable to give credence to this possible fourth dimension, spend their lives waiting for the lifting of that specific veil of necessary lies. There is some wisdom in ignoring the creeping sense of the soon and inevitable stumbling insurmountability of the third step.

Still, my father's back remains a proof of being and extension.

It's funny how I am now moved to tell myself that he knew I was there. At nine or eleven or thirteen, it was of the utmost import that he not detect the nose-breathing spy outside his door. What I thought then to be of the silence, I am now proving was no such thing. These exposures only work in retrospect, I suppose, when you realize just how clear the coast has always been.

Still there is something missing, a more primordial link.

I have often and truly joked, while in the bliss of scratching a purring cat or an attentive dog behind the ears, that all inter-mammal relations are based on giving head . . . People just take it different, that's all. For us it has become religion. It is a prayer to ecstasy, a disclaiming act, a muffled cry of God.

I find myself again in my parents' bedroom, leaning back on the cherrywood chair, the two enormous long-haired tom cats, Black and Wenge, swirling between my legs, jumping up on the dresser, nuzzling my nose with theirs. This is my mother vision. I am an ageless child, leaning back on the chair. She is cocooned in her myriad of blankets and pillows, crumpled Kleenexes sprout from her fertile bed. It was here, I think, that we became friends, in that first and uncomplicated way. This is how I picture her, the vision I hold when my phone rings and it can be no one else . . . and always the sun gleams through the rounded window in this homescape of my mind.

Still, it's difficult to establish or even re-establish intimacy by telephone. There are hotlines and psychics, of course, and with them those willing to believe. Willing themselves to settle for being touched in that way, for whatever amount. Then there is meeting someone again and seeing a certain new light in their eyes, a beam you believe is affixed to you. There are messages on machines, can't really talk now re-calls, blind silences . . . because it is the light that you are both seeking, the light that can never be seen through this medium or that device.

But then you take old Joe Campbell, immortally dead these 15 years. He still seems like such a nice man, so able to connect, describing the perfect courage of the soldier acting beyond thought, relying on the underlying, that which reverberates, transcends the circuitry inside. All this despite the medium, the constant PBS pledge-drive interruption, the impossibility of actual touch or answered question . . .

With this my loop returns, if it ever left, to the crack in my parents' bedroom door, the space between the hinges, my father's back, the sense of enduring weekend mornings that speak of French toast.

"What are they looking for?" my father hisses into the thin air as another car, Sabbath-clean, revs its engine under the foot of the necrophobe inside. I spy my father in crisp slow motion as he unclasps his hands and places them on the sill of the rounded window.

"What are they looking for?" he asks again, looking for archetypes and ending up with animals in the light sublime.

"They're never going to find it," he finally answers, all the malice gone from his voice.

Yet, there remains that light between us, this light in which I see his perfect courage, always thinking, completely afraid and utterly alone.

THE FAT GYNECOLOGIST

"More! More! More!" Paulo screams, his mouth wide open, his fists pumping, the flab on the underside of his arms pounding the back of his neck, waves of fat cascading across his shoulders. "Give it to me, baby!" as loud as he can. "MOOOOOORE!"

He throws his head back, still yelling full force, and swallows the tequila Julie is pouring down his throat straight from the bottle. It never touches his lips. Chantale is just finishing up her second song, barely showing any tit at all. Tony and Filipo are supporting Paulo's chair down low even as Julie puts the Jimenez bottle back in her holster. The boys hoist Paulo back into an upright position. As she leaves, Julie makes sure to brush her floppy boobs right up against Paulo's fat face. He tries to get a lick in, but he's too slow. She walks away, giving him a wink. He gets hard as a rock. He remembers his birthday, that time in the booth . . . Jesus Christ, he thinks, with all the T and A I see, that's the one that fucking gets me, that fat ass, those tits down to her ankles . . .

Paulo looks towards the door. The big-ass black bouncer in his fucking Matrix battle-shirt is there, no one else. Paulo slowly cranes his thick neck all the way around, taking the whole place in — the three tables of Chinese guys in nice suits, young fuckers too, and there's a pretty good dyke scene playing on the TV in the corner, a blonde and a brunette with a big-ass dildo. The sound is off, but Paulo is lip-reading their moans, he's hearing the action like he's in the room with them. He's also hearing the college kids sitting behind him and getting kind of irritated. Who do they think they are? Some kind of a fucking team? He's out of the movie completely. One of them, one of those college kids with their college bomber jackets, seems to be talking to him.

"Excuse me, is someone sitting here?" The kid's got a goofy-ass grin on his face.

Paulo gives him a dirty look and turns his 365 lb. body all the way around so as to give the kid his big back. "Where the fuck is fucking Mikey?" he yells in Filipo's face.

"I'm not that animal's fucking keeper."

"Some fucking kid wants his spot. Could you fucking believe it? Asshole."

Mikey's spot, dead centre of Gynecology Row, is always Mikey's, even when he doesn't show. Not that it really matters for seating purposes. People don't sit right up next to Paulo as he takes up most of the stools on either side of him. Mikey doesn't care though, they're first cousins, more like brothers. Yeah, Mikey is two years younger than Paulo but he's always looked out for him. That's just the way it is. Mikey is smarter than him, better-looking, tougher . . . he's the gifted one in the family. But that's not all there is to Mikey. Mikey is so great because he is always putting other people ahead of himself, never blowing his own horn. Paulo smiles, thinking of how when Chantale's third set is over he's going to tell Tony and Filipo all about the time Mikey got back-to-back blowers at that place up near Ste. Agathe.

The lights flicker and the MC cuts in, "And now, gentlemen, put your hands together one more time for the beautiful, *la belle Chantale*. A reminder, gentlemen, that all our girls are available for five-dollar table dances or the ten-dollar full-contact private dance where anything can happen, *presque . . . Encore un fois, la magnifique Chantale!*"

The music starts pumping, loud hip-hop, Paulo doesn't know what the fuck band it is. He can dig the beat, but he still misses the old days when the third song would be something slow, usually Phil Collins' "In the Air Tonight" or that song from the movie, what the fuck was it called, Rachel Ward is really hot . . . whatever. It made them dance sexy, lots of squirming around on a bearskin or strip of shag carpet. Lots of pussy play.

Chantale isn't dancing slow, she's moving with the beat. She has her panties off at least, but she's still hiding her tits. Paulo doesn't get it, they're the best things she's got, 38 D at least and real as far as he can tell, which isn't too good because she's still got them covered up. Is she saving them for a private dance? She does a pretty good turn down the pole and lands right in front of Filipo, doing the splits. Paulo leans in and howls. Tony and Filipo howl too. Chantale slowly glides a finger from between her legs all the way up to her pouting lips. She extends the finger and Paulo takes it in his mouth. It's out before he knows it and Chantale is across the stage in a hip-hop beat.

"Lip-to-lip service," Paulo screams and runs his thick tongue over his swollen lips and most of his goatee. He takes another look around the room for Mikey. Not at the door. Not at the bar. Not there. Maybe he's in the dressing room. They always let Mikey in the dressing room. Paulo's watery brown eyes are no longer looking for Mikey. They are set on Julie's huge ass. She's pouring shots for the Chinese guys and laughing. The bottles are rattling on her belt. She stands up straight and reties the knot on her T-shirt. Paulo wants to bury his face in her chest. Just as she finishes the knot, she looks over her shoulder, right at him and winks.

The music fades.

"A big hand please, gentlemen, for *la belle Chantale . . .*"

Paulo turns to the stage and raises his hands over his head. He yells full tilt and bangs on the stage as Chantale makes her way off. He turns to the crowd behind him and tries to get them into it. The applause gets a bit louder and a couple of the college kids start to hoot. Chantale scurries back to the dressing room clutching her shoes, panties and her little black purse to her big chest. The house lights come up a bit, Paulo scouts the room again. He looks for Julie, she's not there. Another quick scan for Mikey. Nothing. Two business types at the door digging in their pockets for the cover charge, that's it. The idiots behind him are talking loud shit again, giggling like little girls. He gives them his back. Where the fuck is Mikey? He's gotta get here before . . .

"*En dix minutes, messieurs, notre grande spectacle,* all the way from Dusseldorf, Germany, *Vedette des nombreuses filmes de fesses,* former Olympic discus thrower, reigning domination queen, Mistress Ava Brawn."

Now's the time to go into that thing up north, Paulo thinks, turning towards his guys.

Filipo leans and cuts him off. "You wanna do a booth before the show?"

He considers for a moment. He really wants to get into the Ste. Agathe story, how skanky most of the bitches were . . ."I'll wait."

"For what? Get you revved up for the show, fuck. Nig's paying," Filipo presses.

Paulo leans across him, his belly ruining the crease in Filipo's pants. He puts his hand on Tony's knee and says, "That true, Nig?"

"Which one you want? You fat piece of shit."

"Who the fuck is left?"

"Amber, the black chick, no offence, Nig," Filipo says, trying to shift under Paulo's weight. He manages a position where he can breathe and continues, "Chantale's coming out of the dressing room . . ."

"Okay, I guess. I mean, I gotta see her tits, right?" Filipo and Tony push Paulo back into his chair. Filipo takes a deep breath. Tony signals Chantale. She's coming over, swinging her little black purse and making secret eyes at Paulo.

• • •

Mikey had entered through the "exit only" door that leads from the alley off the parking lot directly into the dressing room. He'd knocked once, real hard, and said, "Candy." The door couldn't have opened faster. He'd exchanged pleasantries with most of the girls. Melanie had shoved her tongue halfway down his throat and made a for-real grab at his tool. Maybe she thought he'd cut her a rate. Maybe he would, but he doubted it.

He's been waiting to see the big star for fifteen long minutes. Long because of the two lines he'd done on the dash of his 300zx out in the parking lot. Long because, as she'd changed between songs, Chantale whined to him about the bar, the customers, the music, the sound system, the quality of drugs available, life in general . . .

"If my cousin talks to you, just don't tell him you've seen me, alright?"

"The fucking new DJ doesn't know how to set levels . . ." She has a voice like a bird that became extinct because it had such a lousy voice. The price of doing business.

"Are you listening to me?" he snapped.

"Sure, don't tell the fat guy you're here. What do you think of the new DJ"?

As soon as she'd left, Mikey took another little toot just to get over her. He cut a couple of lines on the glass-top counter in front of the make-up chair.

I am one bad-looking dude, he thinks, admiring his reflection in the mirror. I am one good-looking man. Chiselled features, full lips, deep black eyes, neatly trimmed goatee. When he'd boxed, he'd been a middleweight, then he got into the bodybuilding and bulked up too much. He's too short to pull it off being a welterweight or light heavyweight. Not enough reach. He'd been a hell of an erotic dancer though. Steroids never shrank Mikey's balls. How long is this bitch going to make me wait?

Julie comes into the dressing room peeling off her liquor-soaked T-shirt. She sees Mikey looking at her through the mirror. He's smiling and waiting for her to come over. She throws the T-shirt on the floor, unhooks her booze holster and slings it over the back of a chair.

"Could you pass me the deodorant?"

"How long are you gonna make me look at those things?" Mikey gives a look of disgust followed by that fucking grin.

"Can I ask you something? Why do all you guys have that same fucking beard? Is it some kind of Portuguese thing?"

"Who's here?"

"Who do you think? Filipo, fat boy and that nigger friend of yours."

"Don't call him that." Mikey is out of the makeup chair in a flash. His strong right hand is on Julie's throat. "Tony's not a nigger, his mother is fucking Brazilian. You got that?"

"Jesus. I get it." Julie tries not to flinch.

Mikey's hand makes its way from Julie's throat to her left breast. He traces a line across her heart. He cups her gently, making her nipple go hard with his thumb and forefinger. "Where's my manners?" he says. "Take a line."

"Fucking psychopath," she mutters.

Mikey smiles, all clean and white.

Julie takes the rolled-up American $100 bill he'd left on the counter and bends over to do a line. Mikey is behind her with both of her breasts in his hands. His hips are grooving to Destiny's Child. Julie feels his thick penis through his thin chinos and that hard metal on his hip. She does two lines fast and leans back up, arching into Mikey and turning her head, her eyes closed, her mouth slightly open.

Mikey is whispering in her ear, "You wanna do me a favour? Is that what you want?"

"Yes . . ." she whispers back, her tongue searching for his in the dark and flashing lights behind her closed eyes, in her exploding brain . . .

"You wanna go ask Miss Star Attraction to come out here? I gotta talk to her." Mikey spins her around. Julie's head is still swimming in sex and cocaine. He has his hands on her shoulders. She opens her eyes and he's wearing his wicked little grin. "And why don't you put a T-shirt on or something? Fuck. "

"Cocksucker."

"Who, me or you?"

"It was a hand job."

"That's not what I hear."

·   ·   ·

Chantale is nasally humming along to Destiny's Child. Her feet are wedged into the corners of the mirrored door, propping her body up against Paulo. His fat fingers are massaging her ass; his beard is tickling her new improved 38 Double D's. She feels the moisture of his saliva on her nipples. She grinds her hips into his belly. Her eyes are a million miles away. She's thinking about the gram she'd just picked up off of Mikey, imagining it in the tiny darkness of her purse. She's glad she didn't do a line; if she had her nipples would be killing her, not just kind of wet and hurting.

Paulo's mind is flashing all over the place. He's thinking about Mikey, all the strippers Mikey's fucked, picturing Mikey doing it, wishing Mikey was seeing him now with Chantale. He's hearing those fucking jokers who were sitting behind them, all the fucking jokers he's had to deal with over the years, him and the boys kicking some ass, getting pissed, Julie and him in this same booth . . . That's the picture he wants, that's what he wants to be seeing, that's what he wants to be hearing. His special birthday present from Mikey.

His pants are totally off, his thing is hanging out the front of his XXXX-L boxers. Julie swings the door open and steps in with a big smile on her face. She's got flakes of blow all over her upper lip and smells of booze and hot oil. She takes off her top and flings it in his face. She's down on her knees, trying to spread his legs. He feels his underwear start to split. He lifts his buttocks off his seat as best as he can and Julie yanks his shorts down hard and fast. It's enough to get them over the hump.

"There it is," she says.

He feels her hand grabbing it. He closes his eyes and lets out a roar. Next he feels her tongue, it's gotta be her tongue. It's warm and wet and flicking lightly right on his tip.

"Hold on a sec," she's saying, lifting his belly on to her shoulders, trying to find a way to get at it properly. She's touching it again, but with what? It feels like her hands, warm with oil, but Paulo isn't sure. Maybe it's her mouth. He tries to look down to see what's happening, but his stomach is in the way. Even in the mirror he can't see anything but his over-hang on Julie's head. He tries to shift to maybe get an angle, but he can only see it in his mind. She's making sucking noises, but she's also talking, saying, "Ooh baby" and "It's so hard." How can she be talking so much if her mouth is full? He closes his eyes and lets it happen. In his mind he can see her giving him head, can feel her tongue . . . that's what counts.

And then it's all over.

The music has stopped. Chantale is climbing off of him. She wipes his drool off of her chest with a small stack of wet naps. She's asking him in that terrible voice if he wants another dance.

"We got time before the show?"

"Two more songs."

"Sure, what the fuck," Paulo says, handing her a $20 bill.

•   •   •

"So is she going to do it?"

"That's what she says." Mikey smiles and pats Julie on the ass. "Weird chick. I had to pay cash. I gave her two bills, you'll never guess what she did with them."

Julie is putting on her holster. She'd checked the levels on the bottles when she got back from the bathroom. The vodka was three ounces low. If he didn't say anything about the blow, she wasn't going say anything about the booze.

"I better head back in. You coming?"

"I'm gonna watch the beginning from the window. Don't tell them I'm here, alright?" Mikey slips her a $50 bill. "Give 'em a couple of rounds though."

"Real subtle."

"Tell them they're on the fucking house."

Julie shakes her head and kicks the swinging door open. She's all attitude and ready to go.

So is Miss Ava Brawn, all 6'1" of her muscular body elevated an additional 8" by her spit-polished, calf-hide, stiletto boots. She's wearing a leather halter and mask, matching cruel-looking studded gloves and collar. She carries a whip. The MC is moaning her name in a showy crescendo and German industrial music is pounding out from the speakers. Paulo screams his lungs out. He beats the stage with his fists. The college kids are hooting like a pack of hicks.

Julie grabs Paulo by the hair and pulls his head back. She's taken the nozzle off of the bottle. Tequila spills all over his shirt and face, gets in his eyes, up his nose and he loves it. Mistress Ava Brawn is rubbing up against the pole and whipping her hand. Her biceps have been oiled and they gleam in the flickering red and green light. Paulo violently shakes his head from side to side, sending a rain of tequila to the four winds.

He wipes his mouth with the collar of his shirt and tries to get into the show. She's hot, as far as he can tell, but she hasn't even taken her mask off. The music sucks too. Where the fuck is Mikey? The tequila is starting to hit. He takes a couple of deep breaths and then the first song is over and nobody's seen nothing yet. He thinks about getting up and going to the can, just to splash some water on his face and catch his breath. He starts to rock his way out of the chair. The college kids are laughing and Mistress Ava Brawn hasn't left the stage. She goes right into her second song. Paulo settles back in, what else can he do?

Good thing, too.

Just as the music cuts in, she's right there in front of him. She bows her head all the way down, letting her long blonde hair touch the floor. When she arches back up, flipping the mass of hair behind her, she is no longer wearing the mask. Two of the big steel buttons on her halter are undone and Paulo can clearly see the contours of her breasts, the hint of her nipples. She plants her boot on his forehead. Her panties are hanging from the toe, he tries to jerk his head back and make a grab at the panties with his teeth. Ava's foot pushes him back in his chair.

Paulo roars.

•   •   •

Mikey slides around the back of the room, stations himself at the bar and takes it all in, every detail, danger and opportunity. His eyes are all pupil. Everyone else is moving in slow motion, he can hear every word they say. "$6.75 for a club soda?" some four-eyed geek at the end of the bar says. *Janine's got nice legs. Two guys at the door, losers. No one else in this place is packing, maybe the Chinese kid with purple streaks in his hair.* He can see the pores in Julie's skin from across the room. "Fat gynecologist," he hears from the tall blond kid behind his boys. The college boys laugh. Surfer dudes with letterman jackets. What are they, Ski Team? Won't last long. Mikey's biceps flex. He inhales deeply through his nose, picking up some residue. He orders a vodka tonic.

Mikey zones in on Paulo. He's really getting into it, trying to get the crowd going. Mikey lets himself smile, wills his arms to relax. He licks his gums slowly and turns his gaze to his own reflection in the mirror behind the bar. He catches Melanie looking at him. Maybe he'll let her blow him for half a gram.

•   •   •

Mistress Ava Brawn is naked except for her boots and gloves by the third song. She lightly whips both Tony and Filipo before settling on Paulo. "You like it, Piggy-boy?" she says, caressing her whip. "You *vant* some? Is that it? Bend over, Piggy-boy!"

Paulo leans over across the stage. She pulls his shirt over his head. All he can see are the flashing lights reflecting off the stage, and just at the edge of his vision he sees her dangerous spiked heel. It's right there. He can almost touch it. He can feel her directly above him now, she inches closer, he feels her heat approach. It is there. She is sitting on his head. He feels her wetness and something sharp on his scalp. The crowd is chanting. The studs from her glove are digging into the back of his neck. He begins his primal scream before the whip strikes home.

The sound of the whip hitting Paulo's back silences the crowd. Mikey is on his feet ready to do anything. The music stops. The room comes to a halt. Ava Brawn slowly raises the whip and holds the pose.

Paulo gives the thumbs up sign and screams, "YEAAAAAH!"

The whip comes down again and the crowd goes crazy. The ski team starts chanting "Piggy-boy! Piggy-boy!" The Chinese guys and some of the others get into it. The whole bar is rocking. Mikey's eyes get really wide then he shuts them to a squint. He makes a fist. He knows how it's going to go down.

Mistress Ava Brawn keeps whipping Paulo. He begs for more. She's got her knees on his shoulders and is ordering Tony and Filipo to haul him out of his chair. He can feel his pants being pulled down; tiers of fat shudder across the vast expanse of his ass as her whip comes down. Paulo is trying to picture Julie in the booth again, but he's remembering what happened just before that . . .

He'd said he was going to the booth to wait, but headed for the bathroom instead, to get a little water, catch his breath. He should have gone straight into the can, but he was kind of woozy and had to steady himself outside the door. He heard a loud laugh coming from the dressing room, followed by something he couldn't make out and another big laugh. He moved in closer to listen.

"I'm serious. If no one goes for a gram, I'll up it to one and a half." It was Mikey. "Christ, all the favours I've done for all of you over the years . . . alright two. Two fucking grams. You know what that's worth?"

Another big laugh.

"An eight-ball and that's my final offer."

Paulo heard a toilet flush, loud footsteps and a rattle coming from the back of the dressing room.

"I'll do it." It was Julie.

"No way. I promised him a stripper, not a used-up waitress."

"I don't see anyone else taking your deal." Julie made to leave, Paulo turned towards the men's room, his heart racing, unable to breathe.

"Alright, but two gees. You don't rate no fucking eight-ball."

"I can't believe you're going to do it with that pig." Chantale's awful voice had cut right into him. She and Julie came out of the dressing room together, walking too fast and way too wired to notice Paulo was standing right there, trying to inhale, slow his heart, close his ears.

"What the hell," Julie said. "I grew up on a farm."

Mistress Ava Brawn finally stops whipping Paulo's ass. He is sore. She's left her mark. He's let out various excretions, but isn't sure which or when. All he knows is that he's wet. She tightens her grip on his shirt, twisting it tight around his neck. She hauls his face into her groin. She grinds into him. He gasps for air. His tongue is hanging out, tasting her, being cut by her clit ring and the two tightly rolled $100 bills she had unceremoniously inserted into herself right after Mikey had given them to her.

"Suck them out," she screams, giving the shirt a twist. "Piggy-boy! Piggy-boy!"

Mikey glides in behind Tony and Filipo. He puts his hands on their shoulders and leans his head in. "How long has that been going on?" He nods his head back towards the ski team, who are leading the "Piggy-boy! Piggy-boy!" chant.

"All fucking night," Filipo says.

"Why the fuck didn't you do anything about it?"

"Paulo didn't say nothing . . ." Tony starts to explain.

"Besides we were waiting for you, fuck," Filipo adds.

Mikey slowly nods and grins. He turns away from his boys and picks out the leader of the ski team right off. The music fades, Mistress Ava Brawn releases Paulo and strikes a pose. The stage lights go down and the whole room is caught in slow motion by the strobes flashing from the back of house. Mikey walks right up to the team captain, grabs a fistful of hair with his left hand, snapping the kid's head back. He delivers a short, powerful right jab to the kid's throat, crushing his larynx. The ski team captain and Paulo hit the floor in unison. Paulo spits out the two $100 bills, sending them careening across the stage and into the audience. They land at Mikey's feet. With the pointy toe of his low-cut Italian boot, he rolls the money towards the ski captain who is curling in on his own pain, choking on blood. Mikey shoots his black eyes at the other skiers, turns on his heels and heads to his seat; dead centre Gynecology Row.

Paulo's face is purple, his tongue is flailing, his heart rate is dangerous. He feels a hand on his shoulder. He cranes his neck around and there's Mikey, smiling hard. "You saw . . ." he gasps.

"I wouldn't miss it for anything." Mikey's ultra-white smile and black eyes shine.

• • •

Mikey kisses Paulo's cheek and leaves him on his bed, drunk and sleeping heavily on his stomach. He grabs his stash from behind Paulo's dresser, puts Paulo's soiled clothes in the laundry hamper, turns off the lights in the bedroom and cuts himself a line in the bathroom. What a fucking night. He'd have paid a grand for that show and he almost got his two bills back. Holy fuck, that look on Paulo's face . . . it was worth anything. Mikey does his quick line and checks himself out in the mirror. Perfect. He inhales deeply and heads back into the night

The welts on Paulo's backside rise like angry mountain ranges. The rhythm of the throbbing in his bruised, fat-encased trachea lulls him to sleep. He is too far gone to be disturbed by the high whistle of air struggling to escape from his collapsing lungs.

Paulo's mind flashes through images of Julie's ass, Chantale's breasts, the cruel proximity of Mistress Ava Brawn. It was the greatest night of his life. The best. Better than hearing about all the strippers Mikey has done, better than the booth with Julie, better than anything. Everyone watching him, chanting for him, giving him a standing ovation. Paulo is filled with love, for Mikey, his boys, the bar . . . his eyes well with tears.

He blocks all the bad things, the ones trying to creep in — the way chicks were talking about him, the idiot college kids and all the things they had said, all the things he pretended not to hear, the way people fucking *are,* all the bullshit you have to take in life. He didn't want to think about it. Not everybody is like that. Some people are different, some people are just better, like Mikey.

That's it.

Paulo fixes his mind on that final moment when he looked over and Mikey was there. That moment when she'd let him fall, that incredible release and he'd looked for Mikey and he was there and smiling. He'd seen. With that light squeeze on Paulo's shoulder he'd let him know that he'd seen everything, set the whole thing up, given it to Paulo as a present.

In that final moment between consciousness and his final sleep, Paulo feels the pain slowly ebb away. His final breath is a sigh of gratitude for Mikey's special gift.

THE WAGONEERS

*R*osalie couldn't understand what was taking so long. How hard is it to find a ski jacket? Especially since it was probably the only one back there among the trench, over and greatcoats. The coat-check girl had tossed off her bright, practised smile and had come back empty-handed, shaking her head. She then served two more customers before taking another look. Now she's coming back again, shrugging her shoulders, indicating her obvious lack of success.

"Are you sure you left it here?"

"Well, I gave it to my friend . . ."

"I'm just not sure this is our ticket. I mean it looks like one of ours, but . . ."

"I did drop it in . . . the sink. So it got wet. I thought the number looked clear . . ."

"Maybe you or your friend got this ticket another night and you, you know, found it in your pocket. Or your friend did. That happens sometimes. You should go ask her again."

Rosalie had double-checked with Heather, but still, it might be her fault or Heather's. It was Rosalie's habit to blame herself first (things did usually end up being her fault, after all), but the ticket she gave the girl couldn't have been from another night, as Rosalie had never been here before. It was also doubtful that she'd confused it with a ticket from another bar since she almost never went places where you check your coat. She almost never went anywhere. Besides, Heather had another ticket, presumably for her own coat, which was the twin of the one Rosalie was trying to give the vacant-eyed coat-check girl.

Rosalie was finding this encounter frustrating, but hardly surprising. These sorts of things always happened to her. The cashier at the supermarket always had to count her register just as Rosalie's turn came. She got head lice twice in elementary school and she loses her glasses constantly, as if she didn't have enough trouble fitting in, as if she weren't blind enough even with her glasses on . . . but this was different. For once, things seemed to be going her way — she'd actually met somebody, had a real conversation with him. When's the last time that happened? Never. She was swimming in emotions she didn't know she even had or was allowed to feel . . . and now this.

She was about to explain all of this to the coat-check girl, but the smile had already been flashed and the long, pretty back turned.

"It's sort of a ski jacket, navy blue with pink triangle thingies on the sleeves." Rosalie is describing her jacket to the back of the coat-check girl. "Maybe somebody tucked it under something, it is bulky . . ."

She's already getting someone else's coat, giving them her bright, empty smile. Rosalie almost says something. Is her impatience starting to show on her face? When was the last time that happened? But she doesn't say anything. She shuffles her feet and adjusts her glasses. Maybe she should forget about her jacket. It looks so goofy he'd probably laugh at it anyways. Rosalie tries to put the thought out of her mind. It's too cold outside to go without a jacket and her keys are zipped into its secure inner pocket.

• • •

Ash sat at the bar of the Sweet Onion Lounge squeezing little slices of lemon into the remains of his $4.75 club soda as he watched the after-work King Street crowd file in. He was the first one in. He was never the first one in. The first one out, well that's another thing, that's the whole point, isn't it? The trickle he'd come in on had turned to a flow. The men — mostly middle-aged bankers and businessmen with ruddy-skinned jowls, wearing Brooks Brothers suits, and a few younger, loud-mouthed, middle-management types, decked out in Hugo Boss, telling each other fish stories. The women — lady executives trying to be one of the boys, secretaries looking for a bump in lifestyle, a couple of oddball dental hygienists, and three cute little MBA students taking a glimpse into the future . . . Ash imagined the women, one by one, on the red satin backdrop of his bed.

God, he missed this, choosing the prey, then the stalking, the pounce, the kill . . . he really needed the kill. He wanted it raw and mean, loud and animal. His eyes took in the twenty-one different scotches on the wall behind the bar. Ash lusted. He needed the 12-year, no, 18-year-old Mac-Callum, the very tempting Islay Mist, a slightly orange Glen Morangie. He looked down at his soda and scowled.

"Jesus H, Ash. What is that, club soda?" Vince the bartender was just coming on duty; that's how early it was. "Oh no, this is bad math. I don't see you for a couple of weeks, plus you're drinking soda, equals they got you in the Twelve fucking Steps."

"Not me. I could never give myself over to a higher power."

"So, what'll it be?"

"I'll take another soda, and relax, Vincent, it's just a stupid bet."

"Just a sec, duty calls." Vince grinned, and shimmied down the bar to serve one of the hygienists, the fat one with too much makeup, who was pounding on the bar.

Ash kept squeezing lemons into his soda.

• • •

Rosalie didn't like this place at all. She'd never felt comfortable in bars. She'd never felt comfortable anywhere in her whole life really, but bars had always been particularly distressing for her. She'd never been tested, but she was sure she was allergic to alcohol; even the smell of it made her queasy. All her friends in high school (Beth and, for a short time in the tenth grade, Violet) had tried to make her drink "just a beer," but beer was the worst. It smelled of alcohol and old pee. Rosalie could never bring a glass of the stuff close enough to take a sip.

Watching Heather get uncontrollably drunk faster then she'd thought possible, even for Heather, made things even worse. Heather, who'd she'd become "study-buddies" with in trade school (i.e. Rosalie doing all the work for the both of them), Heather, who ended up saying, "How do you like them apples, I'm working in an office two floors up. Bet I'm making more dineros (obscene oral sex gesture), if you catch my drift. Just shitting you."

Rosalie had known they worked in the same building and had avoided Heather for nearly seven months. There had been a few close calls; one time she locked herself in the stairwell and had to climb up eleven flights before she found an open door. Yesterday, she'd dropped her guard for just a second waiting for the elevator and there was Heather. "Oh my Gaaaawwwd!" There was nothing Rosalie could do.

Rosalie has spent half the night hiding in the bathroom, hoping that by some miracle Heather wouldn't still be there when she got out. But she always was, loudly too. You couldn't miss her. "There you are! You want another one of those?" Heather's gin breath putting tears in Rosalie's eyes from halfway across the room. "So how the fuck are you? Would you check this place out? You want to meet the kind of guy where you never have to work another day in your life? This is the place." She pounded the bar every time she wanted a drink. "Barkeep, another!"

Rosalie is about to say something to the coat-check girl who is finally getting back to her saying, "Yes, can I help you . . ." like she's never seen Rosalie before in her life.

●　●　●

Ash kept looking down at the hygienist banging on the bar, her mascara running, her mousy little friend in the ugly pink dress scurrying off to the bathroom at regular intervals. Maybe she's got some decent blow . . .

He wasn't sure if he should make an opening move, let the room know he's in play. Somehow, nothing seemed right. His instincts weren't sharp; the next move wasn't playing out in his mind like it should. "Sperm backed up all the way to your brain," the boys would say, only that kind of thing didn't happen to Ash. At 33, Ash was the perfect age to accommodate the widest possible range of women. He could consider both the steely-haired lady exec in the corner, who had to be 15 even 20 years older than him. or the three little-girl students who had settled at the far end of the long, curved bar. He's smooth, very good-looking, incredibly successful . . . Ash closed his big grey eyes and tried to decide what to do. He was picturing the little college girls getting into it one at a time, then all together, the ugly hygienist begging for more . . .

Jesus, he needed a drink. What was wrong with him? He'd only been gone three lousy weeks; lousy being the operative word, but it was like he'd never been here before, like he'd never delivered an opening line. If only he had a drink, if only he hadn't made that stupid bet with Erik, if only he hadn't blown it so badly, if only Erik hadn't shown up in the first place, if only Erik would have left Ash the hell alone.

If only.

•   •   •

When Rosalie was ten, she first became aware that she stood out like a sore thumb. She had suspected it as early as kindergarten, but all the evidence pointed to her being totally invisible. In the fifth grade things began to change. It was a natural evolution, as the kids around her matured from that state of basic innocence to the pedestrian maliciousness of tweendom . . . socialization as we know it.

For Rosalie, it all began with the funny way her mother dressed her and how she styled her hair twenty years out of date, and her glasses — good god, those awful glasses she used to wear. These days it crossed her mind more and more frequently that she left her mother's sphere of influence and the Temple's, largely so she could wear contact lenses. She'll always cherish that day in Dr. Gupta's office, that first time she saw herself clearly in his mirror. She felt like the ugly duckling at the end of the story turning into a swan. Still, she mostly wore her glasses (the lenses dried out her eyes too much), but at least she picked out some new frames and, to be frank with herself (and she usually was), she was still something of an ugly duckling even in the contacts, but less so, not that it really made a difference.

"Do you even see how other people dress?" she had wanted to wail at her mother. "You make me dress like a weirdo because you're a weirdo! Everyone thinks so!"

She knew what her mother would say: "I'm sure no one notices you at all."

Rosalie had these thoughts every time she escaped to the bathroom and had to see herself in the big movie-star mirrors. There was no alternative, she had to get away from the noise and the smoke and Heather, God for-give her, she needed constant breaks from Heather. She'd been talking so loudly, she'd actually made Rosalie's ears ache.

It was the dress she was wearing that brought it all back. She'd bought the dusty pink frock with two small bows on the shoulder on sale at Winners last spring and was wearing it for the first time. Granted, it was a summer dress and it was a cold February out there, but this was her first dressing-up occasion in a long time.

The second time she was in the bathroom, Rosalie realized this was exactly the sort of dress her mother would have bought, would have made her wear to the meeting house. It made her feel 16 again; feel like the ugly doll her mother used to dress-up for the approval of the other Witnesses.

She wondered whether the other kids, the ones who laughed at her behind her back (all of them), were laughing at her clothes or her religion. Her mother had always said, "They don't understand. They only laugh from fear, because deep in their hearts they know they won't be saved."

Rosalie, standing in front of the mirror, hating her dress, her haircut, herself . . . had an epiphany. The clothes and the religion are one. All those awful, out-dated pinafores and frocks were bought for her precisely *to* sep-arate her from the damned. It was never meant for her to fit in.

That's how she first dropped the ticket into the sink. It got lost in an epiphany.

The coat-check girl closes the gate between them and disappears into the recesses of her cavernous closet. Rosalie tries to get her attention, but it's too late. She wonders if he's still waiting for her. Should she check? Is he going to be looking for her?

She can't decide what to do.

•   •   •

Ash hadn't seen his brother for nearly twelve years. Erik hadn't changed much, he filled up his neat blue Mormon suit a little bit better, but other-wise looked the same, looked at Ash the same too, like they'd never been apart, like they were still teenage bunkmates. "You're really willing to go for this?" Ash had said. "What's happened to your morals, Elder Young? Isn't gambling a tool of the devil?"

"It's no gamble, Ashleigh. I have faith in you."

"You don't get it, Erik, it's not about the booze. I am not an alcoholic. I know you think that anyone who takes the odd drink now and again is an addict."

"I know the difference."

"I have my Daddy's addiction, brother, I like the ladies. I just don't feel the need to marry them . . ."

That did it, that sanctimonious look came over Erik's face. This could only lead to the inevitable theological debate, or non-debate. What was there to talk about? Ash didn't believe in God and he found Mormonism to be particularly ludicrous.

"There was a time, Ashleigh, when you were at least open to . . ."

"Discussing the futility of proving the existence of God?" Ash had snapped. That shut Erik up. He knew what Ash was talking about.

As a ten-year-old, Ash had spent countless nights drawing up plans for ethereal detecting devices, spiritual radios, prayer enhancers . . . No one but the two brothers understood the meaning of the schematics Ash painstakingly taped to the ceiling of their bedroom. That is until their father asked "honest Erik" about them. It was Erik's testimony that put the switch in their father's hand, but it was also Erik who came to Ash's defence, Erik who lauded his brother's curiosity, who admired his sharp mind and tenacity. It was Erik, the 13-year-old Clarence Darrow à la Brigham Young (who the brothers were descendants of) who'd saved his hide from a serious whuppin' . . .

That did it for Ash's faith, though.

"I know you lost faith in our father, today, Ashleigh," young Erik Young had counselled as they lay awake on their bunk beds late that night, "Don't make the mistake of losing faith in Our Father Who is in Heaven. They're not the same."

Erik, at 35, was no different. He was the same gentle, thoughtful soul, the kind of guy who earns and commands respect as a natural function of human interaction. When they were kids, quick-thinking Ash had resented this in his brother, been jealous of it, until that defence, until it was used for his direct benefit . . .

To get away from the God talk Ash poured himself an enormous scotch. Erik, the poster boy for Mormon sobriety (he'd literally been a child model. They'd also both appeared in a TV ad for the Church of Latter-day Saints when they were kids), took the bait.

Back to booze it was.

"Do you always pour yourself triples?"

"No, and I do not drink every day either. I will concede that I drink most days."

"When was the last day that you did not have a drink?" Erik took Ash's hands in his.

"I lead an active social life." Ash broke his hands free from his brother's grip. "This is ridiculous. I am not an alcoholic."

"Do you give me your word?"

"Will that end this conversation?"

"It will close this subject."

"Then you have my word."

• • •

For Rosalie, going door to door to spread the word was by far the most horrifying aspect of being a Jehovah's Witness. What if someone she knew answered the door? She'd die from the shame. It wasn't that she was ashamed of her religion, she believed in God. And even though she didn't spread the word as she knew she should and was almost certain that she, herself, was not one of the chosen (how could she be?), she still considered herself to be a good Jehovah's Witness.

In the end, it didn't really matter if the person on the other side of the door knew her or not. It was the thought of being seen at all that sent waves of mortal panic through her wiry little body. Those slow-motion seconds before the door opens, when you can hear the person coming down the hall, fiddling with the lock . . . for Rosalie there was no dread like those steps from within. She'd feel like every blood vessel in her body was exploding, and her colour would turn from her usual pale beige to tomato red. By the time the person was actually there in front of her, Rosalie could rarely speak. If she was on her own, her trembling little hand might offer up a copy of *Watchtower,* and that was it. Either the person took the magazine or shut the door in her face . . . transaction over.

"The worst was when I had to go around with my mother," she'd told Ash. "She was really pushy, sticking her foot right in the doorway, making people hear her whole speech."

"Like a vacuum cleaner salesman," he'd grinned.

"Exactly, but most salesmen don't speak in tongues."

"I didn't know you people did that. Well, at least you don't owe the whole faith to a golden salamander."

"It was just terrible. I died and died and died every time. I joined the prayer-house youth group when I was eleven just so I wouldn't have to go with her. I did have to go door to door like more than twice as often, but it was worth it."

Rosalie couldn't believe they'd talked about this stuff. She never told anyone she was a Witness, not that she met many people, well not socially. Of course, there were always Dr. Miller's patients, but they did not socialize with her . . . Yet, here was this incredible-looking man who was actually interested in what she was saying, who sympathized with her.

"I guess Mormons here go door to door too, but where I grew up in Utah, there was a Mormon behind every door so there was really no point in it," he'd confided. "I know what you mean though. You tell people what religion you were brought up in and they never look at you the same."

"That's it! Exactly!" she'd exclaimed; he seemed to know her so well. "They always ask a sort of polite, stupid question and get away from you as quickly as possible. . . So, how many wives do you have?"

"I'll give you a pint of my blood and tell you all about it." He raised his club soda to hers and they'd toasted.

She'd actually made a joke and he'd laughed. They'd laughed together.

All of this is going through Rosalie's mind as she resigns herself to the fact that she never should have tried to squeeze into the cloakroom through the small aperture between the half-door and wrought-iron gate. It was definitely the wrong decision. She'd seen the coat-check girl coming out of a side door. Rosalie followed her and was handed a "Back in 5 minutes" placard, that vacuous smile and, "Could you be a real friend and hang this up for me?"

Rosalie waited 10 minutes before trying to contort her way into the cloakroom only to get herself stuck, but good.

• • •

Deke, Terry and Steve sidled up to the bar at just the right moment. There were still a couple of stools available and a bit of a line was starting to form outside, a line which Ash could have cut to the front of had he showed up when he was supposed to, half an hour to forty-five minutes after the boys, just when they would be figuring him for another no-show.

They pretended not to notice Ash or what he was drinking. Ash's mind was going full tilt. What did they know? Had big-mouth Steve let the boys in? What was the count at? Should he move on the lady exec? His face stayed cool though, eyes straight ahead, lips sealed tight.

"Deke, my man, who's on top of the pole?" he finally said.

"Excuse me, do I know you?" Deke did it like a pro, perfect right down to the slight loss of focus in his eyes.

"After all this time I'm still the man?"

"Look here guys, it's Ash, at least I think it is . . ."

"Where ya been, pardner," Terry drawls.

"I told you to keep it under your fucking hat, Steve."

"What's the biggie? My condolences."

All three of the guys put a hand on Ash's back and leaned in to murmur their sympathies. Ash's shoulders tensed. He wanted to look over at the little college girls, but knew he shouldn't. He wanted the guys to stop touching him, to go the fuck away instead of trying to get him to talk about going back home, about his father's funeral — may the old bastard rot in that hell he so firmly believed in. He wanted to fuck, more than anything he wanted to fuck, the kind of fuck where you don't talk, you grunt, you sweat, you scream . . .

"So, am I still top *coq* or did one of you assholes actually catch up? I didn't think so."

"Actually Ash, we wanted to talk to you about that . . ." Steve started in.

"Not this fucking college thing again."

"We've been doing it since, well, since you left actually. Give it a try at least . . ." Deke backing Steve up, nothing new in that.

"It's so fucking stupid. You idiots have actually been doing your little tables and charts? It's about sex, not math . . ."

"It's a fucking hoot, Ash, besides the math isn't so tough . . ." Terry completed the triumvirate.

"Alright, go over it again for us poor American hicks who didn't go to the University of fucking Toronto and had to settle for a humble degree from an unknown little school called M.I.T." It had come out harder than Ash had wanted.

"Relax, Ash, have a drink for Chrissake. We'll do one little round and if you don't like it . . ." Deke already had his legal pad out. "Alright, Ash, you've been here . . . how long have you been here? The question is: Who's in play? That's the first step."

Ash had scanned the room again. Nothing much had changed. the college girls were starting to fidget a bit, a couple of secretaries might be removed from the herd, but it would be an operation. The boys could pull it off though. The loud-mouthed hygienist was alone again, and the lady exec was doing her own scan of the room.

"The first move should be the college girls," he pronounced.

"There you go skipping steps again, Ash. Speaking of which, what the hell are you drinking? Vincenzo, What's Ash drinking? His next two are on me."

Ash very much wanted to lose himself in a bottle. These guys were his friends? Here were these little college girls, pulling out credit cards in their daddies' names and getting ready to leave and these morons are doing their stupid rating game instead of going after the prize. Why wasn't Ash going after the prize on his own? Why did he let himself get wrapped up in this kind of bullshit?

"So, given the plus-or-minus-one margin of error, depending on the verification of certain assumptions, with bonuses for virgins and Catholics, from left to right your little college girls rate 3.7, 3.2 and a straight up four ," Terry explained.

"And then you square the number?" Ash knew the answer.

"After final determination of the base number, yes. Take another example; the loudmouth banging on the bar is a definite straight up minus five. It's all about bravery points with that one. You want to hear her profile? We're sayin' high-rise, Eglinton West, so far west you'd swear you were in Hamilton; laminated poster of a red muscle car on the wall, menial job, do ungodly things in bed at the prospect of landing a fish like anyone of us as her boyfriend. Deep in her gut she knows this will never happen. Don't you see how sporting this whole thing can be?"

"This whole minus thing is bullshit."

"If you square it you get a positive number."

"Are we going to move on the little girls or not?"

• • •

Rosalie tries to relax in her cramped space, but she can't. What if he comes back into the bar and sees her stuck like this? My god, from the door he could see her underwear. Rosalie knew this for a fact. A couple had come in moments ago.

"Nice undies, grandma," the woman had said.

"Be nice, Claire," the man snickered. What if Ash came back and saw her grandma undies? She could never look him in the face again. His beautiful face, his sharp features, that perfect smile . . . Maybe he wouldn't laugh. Maybe he would gallantly rescue her, break the lock with his long, strong hands, and he would chastise the giggling crowd Rosalie could imagine forming behind her . . . After all, he might not be a believer, but he was a good Christian. Rosalie was sure of that.

"It started at my father's funeral." He had held out his hands for her to take. They were so smooth and obviously talented, fingers that could move with blinding intricacy. "Every fucking Mormon I promised myself I'd never have to see again was there. My little half-brothers and sisters had all grown up good Christians, all sixteen of them. They welcomed me home like I'd never left, like they even knew me."

Rosalie understood exactly what he was talking about. Three months ago she'd gone back to the Temple for the first time since she'd left home. They all talked to her like they'd just seen her last Saturday. All the old crones seemed to know all the details of her life . . . of course they would, what else would her mother talk about?

"How's life downtown? Are you still working for that Jewish dentist? Does he really work on the Sabbath? Have you been trying to teach him the way?" It was terrible. She'd started crying as soon as she got on the GO train at Pickering and didn't stop until Union Station. She cried for her mother who would never be going back to the Temple either, who would be moving into a half-way house for Alzheimer's patients instead. Her mother who was so crazy to begin with that nobody, not even Rosalie, noticed the disease until it became dangerous. She cried for herself too, but stopped abruptly when she was seized by a sense of incredible freedom as the train came to a halt. It was all over. She'd still have to visit her mother, but somehow, she could ignore what she said, blame everything on the Alzheimer's. Maybe her mother had been sick this whole time, who knows? She'd never seen a doctor until Rosalie took her.

She remembers wiping her nose on her sleeve with a new resolve that day. She marched into the underground city. She ditched the ugly cloth coat her mother had given her, which offered neither protection from the elements nor style, and bought the navy ski jacket with the pink triangles on the lapels that she is now trying to reclaim from the locked cloakroom.

Rosalie thinks she sees a patch of blue that might be her jacket sticking out from under a little bench. The bench and floor in front of it are piled high with bags and winter boots. If the jacket is down there, it's probably very wet.

• • •

"Shit Ash, you should lose points for that."

"Go fuck yourself." Ash knew he was right, though. He'd really blown it with the little girls. He had been nervous and distracted, unable to maintain eye contact, and had giggled, actually giggled when ordering them a round. His mind was just working too fast. He didn't care for the hunt, he just wanted the kill . . . that was the whole problem, amateur impatience. What was wrong with him?

"That's no way to get back on the horse, cowboy." Steve put his hand on Ash's shoulder. "Maybe you ought to be the wingman with the next ones."

"Next ones?" Ash sounded . . . nervous?

"We're going for the loudmouth with the big hair."

"Why the fuck would you want to do that?"

"She gives maximum points, partner. She's a perfect minus five. Besides, maybe you outta get back on a pony before you try a horse, if you know what I'm a-sayin'."

"Just drop the cowboy crap."

"Why? You could use it."

Ash turned his back on Steve as he arrived at the bar. "Vince, pour me another soda, would you? And don't skimp on the lemon."

Why was he wasting his time with these guys? He liked Deke, he guessed, but knew him through Steve, who he knew from work. Terry, who Ash doesn't like at all, came with the frat-boy package. Ash started to wonder if that was what it was all about — not the women, but the other guys, the scorekeepers. Would all his conquests lose their meaning if no one knew about them? No, it was about the lust. Ash could feel it building in him all night. He pictured himself doing it with the lady exec, the little girls he'd giggled in front of, even the perfect minus five the boys were charting out. He started to wonder if they could sense his . . . desperation? Good god he *was* desperate.

"So, you want to be my sober wingman," Deke asked.

"Sure. How much is the mouse worth, by the way?"

"She's a perfect zero," Terry said coming over Ash's shoulder. "Your assignment, should you choose it, is to act as a diversionary device, thus allowing agent Deke to hit his target. Anything else that transpires will be strictly a mission of mercy."

·   ·   ·

Worse things can happen to you than being stuck. They can tear your dress trying to unstick you, laughing at you the whole time. They can offer you a drink, which will just make you sicker, and then they can refuse to accept your refusal of the drink and try to force brandy in your face. Rosalie thought she was going to cry. They all thought she was going to cry, and that's why they hustled her into the manager's office. She didn't cry though. She didn't want any apologies, drinks, coupons or taxis called. She especially didn't want to be sitting in some office while the manager went to see if they could scrounge up some hot chocolate and maybe something for Rosalie to wear.

Worse things can happen.

"I didn't even wait for the funeral service to finish. I excused myself to no one in particular and headed back to the house, my old room. It's someone else's now, one of my little half-brothers, I suppose. Do you know, I don't know most of their names?" Ash was holding her hands, looking her right in the eyes. "I thought that if I just stood there I would feel . . . safe? I don't know . . ."

"But you didn't," Rosalie had ventured, trying with all her might to hold his gaze, to not give in to her weakness and look away, stare at her ugly shoes.

"All I felt was anger. So in the end, I just got piss drunk and passed out on a ten-year-old's bed."

"That's awful." Rosalie had actually begun stroking the back of his hand. Ash suddenly recoiled, her heart stopped.

"I'm sorry," he said, taking her hands again. "I'm not telling you the whole truth and I feel that I should."

"You don't have to tell me anything you don't want to."

"I want to. You're the only person here who would appreciate it. I skipped a part of the story. My brother Erik, the reincarnation of Brigham Young himself, caught me drinking in our old room. He comes in saying: 'The Prodigal returns to his bunk bed.' I tell him I'm not the prodigal son. He was a failure. I am not a failure, I am a success. I am too, I'm a hardware designer," he said, taking a sip of soda

"You mean like hammers and saws and such?" Rosalie asked.

Ash laughed out loud. Containing the club soda through the laugh gave him the hiccups. If it was Rosalie, it would have been streaming out of her nose, she was sure of that.

"I gotta watch out for you, (*hic*) Rosalie, you're a card."

Rosalie giggled at his hiccups. "I've got a cure that always works. Close your eyes and listen to my voice. I'm going to count down from ten slowly. I want you to count with me in your mind. Ready?"

By the time Rosalie reached four, Ash was smiling, his hiccups gone.

"And a hypnotist too. I'm really must watch myself around you."

"You were telling me about this fight with your brother. It's why you're drinking soda?"

Her question hung in the air. She couldn't believe she'd been so forward . . .

"I promised him . . ." Ash began, his eyes once more looking directly into Rosalie's, ". . . I promised I wouldn't drink while I was there and I couldn't even wait until the funeral was over . . ." He looked sad and very vulnerable for just a split second, and then something else. Rosalie wasn't sure because she'd never experienced it first hand before, but if TV and the movies were at all accurate . . . he looked like he was going to kiss her. Should she lean in? Close her eyes? Open her mouth? She was overcome with a feeling she couldn't identify. Was it lust? She felt a stirring in her loins, her face flushed, she was unthinkingly touching herself . . .

The manager comes in with a triumphant look on his face. He's got her jacket and some kind of sweatshirt with the bar logo on it tucked under his arm.

"We're working on getting you some pants or a skirt or something. We'll have you all fixed up in no time."

"Thank-you," Rosalie mumbles. She doesn't like the way his moustache curls when he smiles at her.

"I couldn't find any cocoa. Would you like some coffee?"

"Do you have decaffeinated?"

"I'll go have a look."

· · ·

"Hey ladies, me and my fellow-millionaire-cowboy-jet pilot-buddy were wondering if we could whisk you off to Paris tonight," Deke said, leaning over the little mousy one, speaking right into the fat one's ear. She laughed and he started whispering his pitch, touching her hair, kissing her earlobe. Heather gave back as good as she got, and the next thing you know the two of them are actually making out right there with the little mousy girl in the pink dress trapped between them. Ash put his hand on Deke's shoulder and pulled him off.

"Yeah, catch you on the flip," Deke said to Ash. He winked and led his prey away. The 90-second pick-up done to perfection.

"I'm sorry about that, my friend is . . . a bit much, but . . ." Ash said.

"My friend is very drunk," Rosalie said, trying to straighten her dress and knocking over her soda instead. She looked like she was going to cry, but let out a nervous little laugh.

Ash smiled. "Here, let me get you another one. What are you drinking?"

"Nothing. Soda. I'm sorry," she said to the floor.

"I'll leave you alone if you prefer . . ."

"I think I should go to the bathroom." And off she went to the bathroom again. Ash asked Vince what she was drinking and was happy to buy another round of club soda, slipping Vince a twenty and letting him keep the change. By this time the Onion was starting to hop in earnest. New possibilities sauntered through the door in a steady flow; a parade of Chanel suits and Feragamo shoes. Two secretaries had broken off from the pack and were in a twittering waiting pattern down by the back bar. The lady exec checked him out, he checked back. It looked good, the juices were starting to flow. He was back in the game . . . so what was he still doing there when the little mouse in the wet pink dress came stumbling back looking like she'd just seen the Holy Ghost himself?

"I got you another soda."

"Bless you," she said. Who says that?

"I couldn't let my fellow wagoneer drink alone," he smiled, and that was it — he was in.

• • •

Maybe Heather was right.

"I'm very psychic, you probably remember from school," Heather had drooled confidentially into Rosalie's shoulder. "I know the type, he's a total shark, just look at the way he looks at the room. If he stops moving he'll die. Trust me . . .this is a good sign if you want to get some."

Those signs didn't seem so good to Rosalie. What did Heather know? All the bad signs in the world hadn't stopped her from taking off with Ash's friend, disappearing for almost an hour without saying "boo" and coming back smelling like . . . well . . . Rosalie guessed sex, after all that is what she'd seen them doing in the bathroom, which led to the second dropping of the coat-check ticket, luckily this time only to the floor.

On the bright side, it probably gave her the courage to talk to Ash. No, shock. She was so stunned by the spectacle of Heather and the other man in the bathroom that she hadn't thought to be nervous talking to him.

Then two very frightening facts crept their way into her consciousness: firstly, how was she was supposed to socially interact with this slick stranger, this shark who wanted what from her? Sex? Why would he want that from her? Nobody wanted that from her except for her cousin Peter who once jumped on her and tore at her clothes and had to be pried off of her by his stepfather who strapped him something awful and then put his hand on Rosalie's shoulder to comfort her and she thinks he may have touched her breasts, or rather her little bumps with those pointy, irregular, ugly wrinkled brown nipples she couldn't even look at in the mirror . . . but Peter was half-retarded, so what did any of it mean?

Secondly, how was she supposed to talk to him? She had no idea what to say. Then he made a joke about being on the wagon she didn't really get.

"I don't like to drink," she'd finally stammered

"Me neither." He smiled as if to say, "Look at them getting drunk, throwing their lives into the bottle," which is exactly what Rosalie had been thinking and keeping to herself all night.

"I know what you mean," she smiled back at him. "I used to hate the smell of it more than anything, but it's not the smell so much anymore, I can get used to that . . ."

"No, it's what it does to people," he said, still smiling, but serious.

"The way people's eyes get watery and the way it makes them emotional and silly and sad. I always feel so depressed when I come to places like this."

"You feel depressed because you don't fit in," he'd said. She was mortified, violated. He'd seen through her so easily she hadn't even noticed it happening, just as she was beginning to feel . . . what? Acceptable? Real? An actual woman . . .

"You shouldn't. It's not you, it's them. I've known you less than two minutes and I know for a fact you are the best human being in this place, maybe the only one, myself included."

Ash had solved her second problem; she could talk to him forever.

That only left the first problem . . . sex.

"Alrighty," the manager comes back into his office. "I got you a pair of sweatpants. Sorry if they're a little bit big. You just let me know how much you paid for the dress and I'll cut you a check, easy as pie and we'll get you home."

Rosalie takes the sweatpants and turns her back to the manager. She waits for him to leave.

He doesn't.

She puts on the sweatpants.

•   •   •

The Duke of Kent is nice and subdued and Ash is on his own. He made his escape from the Onion and his little roadblock seems to have worked. Thank the Lord for small mercies. He can't face his friends, the smells, the memories, Rosalie's eyes, the goings on in his own mind . . . Christ, he needs a real drink but settles for another club soda. He fiddles with the matchbook she'd given him. He knows what it means and how to bide his time.

At first, it was so easy for Ash, there wasn't any pressure on him. Deke had made his move so quick, no wingman required. Sure he'd ended up talking to the mouse. No. Not the mouse.

Rosalie.

At first he felt sorry for her, she was so nervous and out of place and such an asexual entity that Ash could, what? Be himself? It was a self he didn't show very often to himself, let alone to others. Erik had had no problem seeing the "real" Ash, if that's who it was, but that was Erik who'd known him since he was born, Erik who could see through anyone

He liked that she didn't drink. He'd enjoyed talking religion with her, talking about real things like morality, family and sorrow. The whole thing was so unexpected, so different from any bar pickup he'd been in on in the past. Maybe that was it though, he wasn't trying to pick her up, the thought never really crossed his mind. The whole time they'd talked, his lust had gone into remission. All of a sudden this wasn't some chick he was talking to, but a person. A person who understood where he was coming from in a way his buddies didn't. Couldn't.

Sure, he'd felt like a hero for talking to her, that was part of it, but that soon faded or transformed into a different heroic mode. He sounded like . . . Jesus, he'd sounded exactly like Erik. The way he'd gone on about the culture of alcohol, the insidious effect it had on judgement and morality . . . it all seemed so well argued coming out of his mouth and he had such a captive audience . . .

The real sick thing is he believed it as he was saying it. What was he doing with these so-called friends? Why was he wasting his life? Is this the real me or my brother in disguise? Why is this odd little Jehovah's Witness looking at me like that . . . ?

Then Deke came back.

That smell of fresh sex took hold of Ash and he had to do something. All of a sudden Rosalie was a woman. A chick. Prey. The pornographic images that had been riddling his mind all night returned in a pink wave of Rosalie. Rosalie tentatively removing her awful dress. Rosalie closing her small, colorless eyes, her little hands trembling, her virgin little pussy getting all wet . . .

Ash felt guilty. For the first time in his life he was able to make the correlation between sex and his own shame.

Ash orders another club soda and scans the room again. He plays with the matchbook and looks at his watch. He sees a few "possibles" and even a "probable" among the few patrons of the Duke, but he knows his move is back at the Onion. He closes his eyes and begins his conjuring — the touch of her hand on his, the corner of her mouth as she smiles, the strap of her dress unfolding down her shoulder . . . He leaves his newly arrived club soda on the bar, pays his tab and stalks back into the night with a savage reel of lust playing in his mind.

• • •

The manager had offered to have her dress repaired and dry-cleaned, but Rosalie declined. She wanted the whole night to end with no loose strings. It's not that she's upset, quite the contrary, it has been a good night, better then she could have hoped for. Rosalie likes to encapsulate her memories, see the stories of her life as little parables . . . kind of like the book of Job over and over again, until tonight.

For the first time in her life Rosalie had felt like a woman. Right at the end, when Heather came back, he'd looked at her in a way that she'd never thought anybody ever would. She thought it'd make her feel dirty, like her crazy mother had always said it was supposed to, but it made her feel alive.

Rosalie had no choice but to grab Heather by the arm and drag her to the bathroom. She had to tell somebody, get some advice, pinch herself to make sure she wasn't dreaming and more than anything she needed someone to make her stop hyperventilating.

"Jeez Marie, it's like you've never done it before," Heather belched.

"Yeah, well not really. I'm supposed to meet him out front. He said he needed some air . . ."

"Oooh, he's hot for you."

"I just don't understand . . ." She should have left then. Maybe she could have caught up with him . . . but she didn't. "Do you have your coat-check ticket?"

"Why?" Heather asked in a drunkenly suspicious way.

Rosalie went on to explain that her ticket had gotten wet and the number was indecipherable and since she and Heather came in together . . .

"Why don't you just point it out?"

She should have got out then but, "That would be almost like stealing."

Heather smiled with significant complicity and dumped the entire contents of her purse into the sink. Some of the bigger, bouncier objects, her lipstick, cellphone and compact slid easily down the rim towards the drain. The smaller items didn't fare so well. An ominous mix of Tic-Tacs and birth control pills careened off the stainless steel counter onto the floor. The coat-check ticket fluttered down to Rosalie's feet. She picked it up and studied the number. She started to turn for the door . . .

"So you want some pointers?" Heather's gin breath scorched her eyebrows, her impossibly long nails dug into Rosalie's shoulder. "The first thing you gotta do . . ."

It was probably for the best, the way things worked out. What would she have done if they'd actually left together, even without Heather's advice? Whatever else had happened, she had met a man and felt like a woman and no one could take that away from her. She has a new sweatsuit and her ski jacket with her keys safely zipped in the inside pocket.

• • •

Ash is still the man at the Onion, that's what the boys will be saying tomorrow.

He's made sure to swing back five minutes after closing time. The doorman will let him in, he always does and then he can sidle in and claim his prize. Just when things had seemed the most hopeless, just when it looked like he might . . . just as he had been affecting his escape he'd seen her and it had all come together. Booze or no booze, off his game or not, he had come through. That's what it's all about. Winners and losers. Natural selection.

"You look like a nice girl," he'd smiled, and handed her a twenty-dollar bill. "I need a little getaway time, say five minutes. I was hoping you could think of something, stage a little delay."

"What are you running away from?" she'd gleamed back.

"Oh, you'll know it when you see it."

She handed him the matchbook with her phone number on it. Ash had no need to call. They both knew that. Good thing, too. He needs that coat-check girl tonight. The thought of her is keeping him ablaze. The bitter February wind cutting through his thin, stylish trench coat turns to steam on Ash's hot skin. Maybe he should take her right there in her cubbyhole. He'd just walk right in, pull down whatever coats are left, throw them on the floor and they'd do it like drunk teenagers. He can see it, smell it, ride it like a wave of fire.

Ash gets to the Onion. The doorman points at his watch. Ash shrugs and gives a pleading smile. The doorman holds up two fingers. Ash grins. Two minutes alone with her is all he needs, the tiniest opening to explode into and he can feel it rising. The door opens. Ash steps in and Rosalie is a blue bundle in his arms.

THE LAWS OF NATURE

*T*hey say certain things are immutable. That's what People believe. They have to. Nothing is though.

When someone says something that seems that it might be, They kill him dead in as many ways as possible. People will do that. Even if the truth survives, it changes. Somebody, or a group, or a progression of somebodies or nobodies even, perverts it so profoundly that They actually come to believe it. When it gets to that point, People, just forget about it.

So, I'm walking up an average residential street. It's not really my neighbourhood, more like half a neighbourhood over. There's some overlap. There always is. It's late September, but still summer. Not Indian summer, for-real summer. It's been hot since June, glorious then relentless. The leaves aren't falling from the trees, they're crumbling on the branch. I have a bag of flaccid soccer balls slung over my deeply tanned shoulders. I'm swinging a brutal-looking air pump in my right hand. I'd left the pin in the nozzle. People are always losing those little pins. They never seem to know where to get them. With the hose coiled around the strong arm of a man in his prime, the nozzle looks like a cobra's head.

A middle-aged man in a plain white T-shirt and navy blue shorts is inspecting his dead lawn. I assume it's his by the way he's looking at it, the way his belly hangs out in a proprietary way. He is People. They. His face is too authentic to have been cast by some talent agent. It is a face not of furrows, but lumps. As I pass, his back is to me, his gaze fixed on the yellow remains of his grass. I turn my attention to the horizon. The park is within my sight. I already see the man and his dying lawn as part of my past. People make connections as a function of being. They don't even know it's happening sometimes.

Breaking the laws of nature, the middle-aged man is walking by my side.

"Did you feel it get a little bit cooler just now?" he asks, as in mid-conversation.

"It usually does when the sun goes down," I answer, keeping up my stride.

"The sun sets at 6:23 today." He is genuinely perplexed.

"Well, it's pretty low in the sky."

We are walking right towards it. Our eyes squint and we are forced to smile.

"Usually, I'd agree with you," he continues, "but this year it's stayed hot all night."

"It's bound to break," I offer.

We've come to the intersection. The quiet road bleeds into a major artery. The end of the working-day traffic is torrid and mean. A faded white outline runs from curb to curb, but crosswalks mean nothing in this town. People look for an opening. They make the best of what's available.

"I don't even think it'll rain," he finally answers.

"Is that what they say?"

"Forecast calls for rain on both channels and on the wireless, too."

"They said the same thing yesterday . . ."

"But it passed us by."

Something about the way he says "the wireless" instead of radio makes me think he's older than I'd first believed. In finishing my sentence, he takes my breath away. He checks the eastbound traffic, I check the west. The sun continues its slow, burning descent, huge and orange over the park to the north. Street directions are slanted all over this town. Nothing is due anything, They say. People have to adjust their gauges.

"I have a melanoma," he says, but doesn't complain. "It's nothing serious. I'm waiting to get it removed."

"How long?"

"All summer. It's killed my golf game."

I glance at the back of his cancerous head, trying to determine when People pass beyond middle age and into the other. At what point on that journey do They gain some form of release and come to comprehend the joy of resignation? I resist the urge to put my hand on his shoulder, to feel under the bandage on his neck. If People only knew, They would do the same.

"How are things on your side?" he asks.

"Almost clear. After the black car, one more, I think. Yours?"

"I think the light changed down by the corner," he replies, crowning his head with his speckled arm. "I can't see that far. I know there's an advanced left turn. You'll have to wait for that."

His words hit me like a knife. I had assumed he was coming with me to the park, that we'd be crossing the dangerous road together. I picture myself in my new running shoes, towing this barefoot old man to paradise like he's another bag of soccer balls. Maybe I should let him go it on his own, sink or swim, run or get pulled under. But, given these circumstances, People help. They let him know he's old.

"That cloud maybe . . ." I point vaguely upwards.

"We'll never get anything out of that one, she's moving too fast."

"Well, nothing lasts forever . . ."

". . . But some things never fall," he finishes.

I hear my name being called. The children in the park have been waiting forever. They're just at that age where they love to tell you that They are People, too. They have rights just like you. So there! You have to laugh and smile and tell them that, yes, it's true, but be that as it may, this is no democracy. No matter what They think. People have to accept that.

"It's all clear," the old man says.

I dash into the busy street listening to the children call my name. The bag of balls thumps my shoulder. The cobra's head drags in my wake.

GREY WHORES

*G*reg had been sure the Guy had been talking about the little juice bar down by the reception desk, maybe have what Carolyn would call, "a multi-nutriliscious orangish concoction." Greg can picture her saying it with that quick smile, those blazing little eyes. He and the Guy could look at the toned receptionist in her tight leotards (baby steps really), he'd have his vitamins, pick up a couple of tips maybe . . . *Design you a whole new program*, the Guy had promised. The Guy just appeared over Greg's shoulder as he'd waited for the peck-deck. He brought his swollen lips too close to Greg's ear when he spoke, or rather slowly whispered, like everything he said was a secret, raising a conspiratorial brow, winking at nothing of note, giving an emphasizing shoulder squeeze . . .

The Guy hadn't meant the juice bar at all.

Do you think Arnold drank juice after a workout? Do you? In Bavaria? I don't think so. Beer, that's the key. The Guy's eyes scan for cavesdroppers. *The Vikings knew that.*

I thought Arnold was from Austria . . .

He trained in Bavaria.

Greg didn't want a beer, not in this place with its darkened windows and its pervasive odour of decay. I'm surprised they carry imports . . .

They don't usually, but I make them.

The reason he could make them was pretty obvious. Just look at the Guy, 5'10", 250 lbs, and muscles rippling in all directions. *I loaded six plates on for my squats today. You gotta do squats, man. I'll put them in your program* . . . He probably can't look at his own watch. More intimidating than his size and strength is that maybe-a-little-stupid-

and-possibly-insane set of his eyes. They seem to go in and out of focus in an unpredictably menacing way. It's impossible to know if this is a conscious act. Greg didn't ask or want to know the details but . . .

I buy the beer myself at the liquor store. They let me keep it here because it doesn't take any place in the fridge . . . what are they going to do? The crazy eyes and a muscle-guy contemptuous smile reinforcing the point. *One time, when I was actually here, somebody else tried to order my beer. My beer. My beer that I'd bought. Now, I will say this, it was a new bartender and he probably didn't know . . . I said I was sorry to the guy after. Not the fucking bartender, if he didn't know . . . well, he should have known . . . I mean the other guy.* He puts his callused hand on Greg's forearm. *I mean, buddy who ordered my beer. He took most of the damage and he had no way to know, right? I'm sorry I didn't think of it then. I told him after. I even gave him one, a beer, you know, to smooth things over. Since then, I don't leave a tip . . . but what are they going to do?*

There are certain advantages to being big . . .

Fucking right!

Well, one day, with your help, maybe I can, you know . . . Greg eye motions to the chart the Guy should be filling in, hoping to get business taken care of, finish the beer and say, "Well" which means good-bye, see you around, thanks for the brew. The Guy slowly licks his pencil, even his tongue looks muscle-bound. He lets out a slow, deep breath and licks the tip of the pencil again.

I think you should start with . . . very slowly in that hard whisper, before he pauses and leans back. *I'm going to have to think about this.* He nib licks again, even slower this time. He looks perplexed and gently tucks the pencil behind his ear. He looks at Greg expectantly.

That means I'm going to need another beer.

Greg gets out of his chair stiffly. The workout, his first since college, is exacting an awful revenge on his thighs and the under side of his arms. He shuffles over to the bar and motions for the German beer. The barman shoots him a dirty look and goes about the task in silent indignation. Greg smiles sheepishly, he wants to say . . .

Don't tip him. The Guy is right there, his chin grazing Greg's shoulder. *Don't leave this fuckwad a cent.*

They sit at the bar. The Guy puts the chart on the bar beside him face down. His huge thighs push against Greg's. He flicks off both bottle caps at once and lets out a guttural laugh to highlight the feat. He turns, trapping Greg in his stool, pushing his face only inches away.

You said your name was Schmidt, right? That's German, isn't it?

If you go far enough back . . .

I need to know. He nods vaguely towards the chart, takes a long pull from his beer and nods appraisingly. *You're kinda tall and lean, but you've got broad shoulders, that's a good sign. I can get you thick. We got to start with what you eat. If you want to build bulk, you have to eat bulk. Let me ask you something. Do you like oats?*

I'm looking for more of a fitness and endurance program. I used to work a really physically demanding job and then I got hurt. I'm okay now. I mean, I've done my rehab. The thing is, I've sort of been riding a desk since it happened and now I think I'd like to get back out there.

Greg can feel the Guy's muscles flex where their thighs are touching and he doesn't like the look in his eyes, all wounded and dangerous. Greg readies himself to fight or flee, definitely flee, get around the Guy and go right for the door. The barman is taking a smug interest. No help there. Three young men Greg recognizes from the gym come in. They glance at the bar, notice the Guy is there, Greg is sure of it; they take a table at the far end of the room.

What is it?

I thought we'd made a connection back in the Gym, that's why I invited you for a beer. Other than buddy, who I pounded, you're the only person I've shared my Uberbrau with. The only one.

I thought we were getting along fine.

I suppose . . . it's just . . . forget about it, his whisper going faint. *I'll help you rehab . . . I was just so sure . . .* He slides the chart between them and starts filling in numbers, quieting Greg with a finger-wave promise of forthcoming explanation. Greg regrets even before saying . . .

What were you sure of?

The way you were moving weight, it didn't look like rehab to me. You were letting it all out, man. Either you're a for-real lifter, which you are not, or the problem has to be of the female persuasion.

Greg doesn't say anything. The Guy continues writing, his big hard elbow pushing into Greg's ribs towards the end of each line. The Guy was right. Greg had spent his workout replaying his relationship with Carolyn. Doing his curls he had tasted tears mixed in with the sweat, remembering Carolyn that first day coming to his rescue.

"So, you're my little bird with the broken wing," was the first thing she said. Not looking at his file, but running it through her short-cropped red hair. "Only you're not such a little bird."

He knew she'd win his case immediately. Carolyn had emanated a glow of pure human trust, of fighting Irish, of downright righteousness. Greg had been mesmerized.

Riding the bike to cool down at the end of the workout, he'd pictured their private celebration dinner. A dinner that had ended with room service the following afternoon. Kissing him in the shower, rolling both of them off the bed again and again . . . She was energy incarnate.

We'll start you with a little cardio, treadmill or step-master, alternate; the stationary bike is for pussies . . .

You're right, it is a female problem . . . I mean a woman.

She broke your heart. Fucking bitch. I knew it.

Her name was Carolyn.

With some guys, they want to look better because they're back on the market, but with you . . . arm fully around Greg's neck, biceps cutting into the base of his skull . . . *I just knew. You're not looking for anybody. You might think you're doing the typical new bachelor dance, but you're not. You feel alone and angry. I know about alone. I know about angry.* He nods wisely. *It's been a while . . .*

Three months.

Greg looks into those crooked eyes. The Guy's right eye meets his gaze, his left stares at Greg's chin. The Guy looks deranged, yes, but also somehow real. There is a person in there. A human being who cares. Despite appearances, the Guy might not be a total idiot. Besides, Greg has to talk to someone.

"You never really let anyone know what's wrong, Greg," Carolyn had repeated over and over again that last night. She wasn't even angry. She was resigned. "Even when I was defending you in the settlement, you were so gracious. It seemed to work, I'll grant you that. I saw them soften. You can have that kind of effect on people. You know how to con-nect, Greg, that's what makes you so frustrating sometimes." Greg knew what she was talking about. He'd known all along. There was nothing he could say, nothing anyone could have done.

Look at you. She had you by the balls. I can tell. You're too much of a man for that. I can see that too. We connected, for sure. Have another one. Really . . . have all you want. Was she hot? Licking his lips, *I'll bet she was hot.*

I guess . . .

"I was so nervous last night," Carolyn had said in the hotel room after their first night together. They were eating scrambled eggs. "I don't know if you noticed but I'm not very comfortable with my body. Well I am, but some guys, guys who look like you . . . let's say I've had some bad expe-riences. Most people expect a certain body type and, well, it's not my shape. God, I'm babbling. Save me. You make it so easy. You're so easy to trust, Greg."

Are you kidding, I feel like the luckiest guy . . .

Excuse me?

I was just . . .

I know, buddy. His arm is around Greg again. *I feel your pain. Let's have a couple more, all right, buddy?* Greg can feel the Guy's forearm as he raises the two-fingered order. *It's all right to cry if you want to, man. Don't worry about those fucks from the gym over in the corner. Fucking lightweights!*

Greg tries to focus, but the double-digit alcohol content on the Uberbrau label remains blurry. The Guy is still whispering in his ear but he can't make anything out. It wasn't the sex or her touch he missed. It was her glow. He always felt so safe within it. It washed over him when-ever she came into the room. It never faded. Not even when she came into the living room that last time with her suitcase and he was just sitting there stunned, not even heartbroken yet. What if she was to walk into this dive and see the Guy's humongous arms all over him? Would he feel it? Would he be able to sense her presence with his back to the door?

Maybe you want to talk about something else, eh, buddy? I had this chick one time, Burmese girl. You ever do a Burmese girl? Incredible. I guess you wouldn't go for that, being German. I'm part German, too. Part a lot of other things. I'm a big mutt. I got some Cree in me, like one-six-teenth. It gives me an edge. I can get into the burn. Love the pain. You know what I mean?

Greg tries in vain to shrug the Guy off of him. He'd wanted to celebrate that day, that day of the last suitcase. Earlier that afternoon he'd signed on to go back to working on site. He wanted to surprise her with the news. He'd even booked their hotel room.

I gotta use the . . .

Talk to a man about a horse, the Guy rasps, patting Greg's back. *I know what you're talking about.*

The bathroom is very small and smells like a barn. A regular working man, that's what Greg sees in the cloudy little mirror. She'd fallen for a regular working man; granted, one with a broken wing. Greg thought he could get her back by becoming that again. She'd been slipping away for a while. He just needed her to see . . . what? Some ridiculous show of virility? Why couldn't he just spit it out?

"You miss the whole point, Greg. I was so proud you'd taken up the union cause. You have to know that. I can't believe you'd make such a selfish decision." That's what she would have said, had he given her the chance. Had she let him give her the chance.

Maybe he was selfish. He hated it. He hated wearing a tie and shaking hands and having a desk and a telephone. Of course he wanted to fight the common man's battle. He just didn't have the stomach to fight that way. He wanted to want to. Maybe he didn't have enough real passion for the plight of his fellow worker. Why couldn't she see that that didn't mean he didn't have passion for her?

"The point is moot," she would have said, had he got around to telling her the news. If he hadn't made the mistake of letting her go first. Able attorney Carolyn had her case so well prepared Greg could only silently plead guilty. The union thing wouldn't have made a difference. Nothing would have. Case closed in the opening argument.

I didn't tell her. I didn't tell her any of it. I just sat there hoping . . .

You've been in here awhile. The Guy is suddenly in the bathroom. *My beer is pretty strong. You being from the Fatherland, I thought you could handle it. C'mon, I think I got a couple left we can kill off.* The Guy fast-walks Greg back to the bar, half-carrying him like he weighs nothing.

Greg manages to steady himself. Nothing has changed. The trio from the gym is still in the corner, the bartender ignores them, and the place is still a hole . . . and the Guy is right there, his hot breath on Greg's neck.

Can I ask you something? What didn't you tell her?

What?

You were saying something back there about not telling her about something.

Work related. Nothing really. It's stupid . . .

I don't think so. I look at you and I know you're a working man. You're not like most of those fucking yuppies I got to share my gym with. I look at you and I know you do a man's work. Am I right?

Yeah, I'm a working man.

Does she even work? Let me ask you that. The Guy's hand is on Greg's leg, steadying him on his barstool. Greg doesn't need the steadying any more. All of a sudden everything is sharp and clear. He realizes he's approaching a period of faux hyper-sobriety that a person gets in the middle of a good drink-up.

So, can I ask you that? The Guy presses down on the word *ask*, his left eye making inquisitory contact with Greg's, the right eye on a mission of its own.

She's a lawyer.

Holy Mother of Shit. Each word is excruciating in tone and on Greg's thigh as the Guy squeezes. *She's going to take you for every dime you have.*

She's not that kind of lawyer

That's a good one. The Guy lets out a knee-slapping laugh.

She's big on fighting for the downtrodden. She does mostly immigration now.

Here's another one: Why would you want to screw a lawyer? So you can do to one of them what they always do to us! It's a joke, get it? Seriously, if you want me to talk to her . . . muscles flexing, malevolent grin. *I've done that kind of thing before.*

Look, thanks for the beer.

Relax. I'm just shitting you. The Guy delivers a hard love tap to Greg's shoulder. *The problem with career women isn't their career; it's the way they push you in yours. Am I right?*

"You think you're just a working stiff, but you're not," Carolyn had said, interposing her short, wide body between Greg and the front door. They had just moved in together and had taken to hello and good-bye kisses at the front door. They kissed quickly then Carolyn went right back into it. "Let me at least finish pleading my case. You went to college. You have your Masters in Poli-sci, for Chrissake. More importantly, you have natural leadership qualities. You listen to people, sometimes too much, sometimes you'll just let anyone ramble on. The point is, people sense that you are a listener. My larger point is that you have a responsibility to others and to yourself to use those skills."

So, am I right?

When you put it that way . . .

Listen to me. I know what I'm talking about. I've had so many chicks trying to push my career, you wouldn't fucking believe it. I always tell them, I'm a personal trainer. That means I personally train people personally. I don't want to do a video or be some fucking TV guru. What I do is real.

I just wanted to get back outside, be up high. It's about freedom. Is that so wrong?

That's what it's all fucking about! The Guy closes in; Greg leans into the huddle, feeling a surge of bonhomie. *You said the magic word, brother! To Freedom!*

They raise their thick German beer bottles and drink. Greg does feel freer, despite the Guy's tight embrace. Who was she to tell him what to do? Who to be? If she he didn't think he was sexy after he came home from a day of real work, man's work, then to hell with her.

That's the thing about women. They always want to turn you into something you're not.

You got that right!

It's like you're their little Ken doll. They like to dress you up. They like to make their little plans. They think a man is going to sell out who he is. I don't think so. Some men do, but not real men. Not you. Not me.

To us!

They raise and touch bottles again. Greg pats the Guy's broad back.

It's amazing, you know more about me in the what, two, three hours than she ever could. . . in two and a half years.

I knew more in five minutes. You have to understand the female mind. It doesn't matter who you are, they try to turn you into their little Mr. Perfect.

All of them? Greg taps the Guy's shoulder playfully.

All of them. Let me ask you something personal. I feel I can do that, because I feel we've connected. He doles out a friendly head-butt. Greg butts back. *Was there another man involved? Don't answer if you don't want to . . .*

Yeah . . . but she didn't really start up with him until after . . .

That's what they all say. You knew though.

I was losing her. I stopped . . . she thought I stopped needing . . .

Whoa, that's okay, brother. We never stop needing. That's what makes us men.

No, you're right. We don't stop.

But what the fuck does our need mean to them? Right? I ask you. Nothing. It's the way of the world, brother. Man provides for woman's needs. He hunts, he works, he kills. But, we're real men here. Modern men, right? We can admit we need. Am I right?

How could she think I didn't . . .

Look at you. You're still hooked on her. You've probably been thinking about her all night, wondering if she might stop in at this place for a drink. You just want to be in the same room with her, don't you?

I will not be her victim! That's what she wants, a fucking victim. I think she just loved me for my shattered fucking scapula. Her little bird with a broken wing. I'm no little tweety-bird.

Fucking-A right!

You know when I first met you . . . Greg smiles and wipes the sweat from his brow. No, forget it.

What?

Nothing. It's stupid. You know that connection you were talking about . . . At first, I gotta admit I didn't really see it. But, you're all right, you know that? I feel . . . The Guy's eyes are going wild. Is he going to cry? Kiss him? You look like you want to say something.

I don't want you to take this the wrong way, a lot of people do. I'm not . . . you know I don't like one group of people more than another. My girlfriend is a Paki. I'm serious. I call her my little Paki package. She loves it. Being, you know, what you are, I mean German . . . you must have certain opinions.

Greg starts to shift under the Guy's weight.

Was buddy who your woman left you for . . . is he of the black persuasion?

What makes you think . . . I mean what does that have to do with . . .

Easy brother, I don't mean any offence. I'm an equal opportunity sex machine. I'll fuck any creed, if you know what I mean. I'm just saying there are some people that have some strong, unnatural preferences. If you think about it, they're the bigots, only sleeping with blacks or spics or whatever. Sometimes said deviants try to have what other people consider a normal relationship. You know, just to see if it works. They always go back to black. It's not all dick size, either. You should see my load . . .

It's just from what you said, I thought, maybe . . .

What are you talking about?

You are the victim of a grey whore. You know, a white chick that only digs black dudes. You know the type. She tried you, the perfect example of the Aryan race, and she just couldn't hold it together. Was her boyfriend before you one, too?

The one before me was Latino, I think . . . Look, you're wrong, it's not about . . .

Was she a blonde? Most grey whores are blonde. It makes for better videos, if you know what I mean.

It's about . . .

I fucking hate to see it, though. I mean, it's so wrong. The Guy plants a knowing elbow in Greg's ribs. *I expect it's the same with most white guys. Most of the time, what the fuck are they going to do? They can't say a fucking thing.*

Greg begins to tremble.

Most grey whores are fat. Like being white makes up for being a pig. What I'm fucking saying is, if you see it, a real white man like you, what are you going to do about it?

Greg is picturing Carolyn naked. She is ashamed of her stumpy body. She is in her little cubbyhole of an office, her, "step-down the lawyer-ladder." Under the awful fluorescent light, her skin is so pale her freckles look like rust on snow. It seems so clinical. So cold seeing her like this.

Something is missing. It is her glow. Her radiance. Greg realizes he is seeing her without her soul . . . then he sees a dark hand, a man's hand, cupping her pointy little breasts, the big fingers pinching her barely dis-
cernible nipples. Behind his eyes Greg sees her thin pink lips pushed up
against a dark purple . . .

I ask you, what are you going to do when some big-lipped jungle . . .

Greg picks up his half-full, very thick Uberbrau bottle and smashes it
into the side of the Guy's head.

Are you fucking nuts? The Guy grabs Greg's arm and twists it behind
his back . *Now what are you going to do?* That hoarse whisper is touching Greg's ear. Greg can feel the Guy's spit? Blood? Beer? *I'm asking
you, brother, what are you going to do?*

Greg wildly flails. He tries to squirm out of the Guy's grip, maybe
catch the Guy's head with an elbow, his shin with a weak kick. He no
longer sees Carolyn in his mind, or the Guy, the dingy bar or anything at
all.

The Guy pushes forward and rebreaks Greg's wing.

A Young Faye Dunaway

Meredith reread her ad. She wanted to take it out. She wanted to strangle Janey for making her put it in, but there it was on her screen — "I look like a young Faye Dunaway."

"You got bigger tits," Janey said. "You should put that in."

Meredith didn't, of course. The comparison was bad enough. There's an obvious resemblance, similar facial structure with that high forehead and widow's peak, same body type with the great legs . . . but her eyes don't blaze the way Faye's do. Meredith had always thought her lack of blaze reflected her own inner coldness. She was afraid others might notice it, too. In fact, she was sure they did. The real problem in identifying herself with the actress is that it will draw attention away from the main body of her user profile: her likes and dislikes, her penchant for modern poetry, her everlasting quest for the truth that is total love. More importantly, it's going to get her too many responses from too many creeps. She knew that. Janey knew that. The creeps probably knew it too.

"I'm not all that young," Meredith said.

"You're younger than Faye Dunaway."

"In what?"

"Real life."

"She's such a good actress," Meredith said thoughtfully.

"So?"

"I've just never seen myself as the leading lady type."

"That's the price you pay for being from London, Ontario. I'm going to the can," Janey snorted.

Meredith closed her eyes and pressed "Send." All she could do was wait for the creeps to come pouring in. Did she look more like Faye Dunaway in *Bonnie and Clyde* or *Chinatown*? What was she supposed to do except ignore the ones who wanted the *Network* Faye? She was beginning to have doubts about the whole operation. She didn't feel ready to "Get back on the horse," as Janey put it. Then there's the question of privacy. Janey assured her that the site has tight security, but what did Janey know? The screensaver came on. Meredith quickly jiggled the mouse to get her personal ad back on the screen.

Still no hits.

"You're out of milk, so I helped myself to the vodka you had in the freezer," Janey said, taking a swig from the bottle.

"I thought you went to the bathroom."

"I peed in the sink."

Meredith's face took on a look of dire mortification.

"Take a joke. So, you meet Mr. Right yet?"

Typical Janey. Janey, with her pierced naval and her assortment of tattoos. Janey with her "I'm-an-outrageous-wild-animal-girl-from-back-east-and-don't-take-no-crap-from-you-stupid-ass-hicks" attitude. Meredith needed that Janey attitude. It was her buoy in this sea of vacant-eyed cowboys and she clung to it. "It's the Montreal connection," Janey explained. "It gives us *culture*." If it weren't for Janey, Meredith probably would have tried to kill herself three months ago when It, the thing, the incident, the realization, call it whatever you want . . . when It all fell apart.

Meredith had been teaching English at Manning Junior High for six weeks and had lived in Calgary for just six and a half. Besides Janey, she hadn't befriended anyone since her arrival. She didn't know anyone in Western Canada except for Dirkland and it was just beginning to dawn on her that she didn't know him at all. Some of the men she worked with leered at her or tried to sidle up to her. She let two of them drive her home, but that was it. Both of her drivers had taken scenic routes, giving her the opportunity to behold the mountains. Both drivers decided to take more direct routes as soon as she mentioned she had a boyfriend.

This city had a way of making her feel decidedly small.

Janey didn't know her from shinola, as they say out here. It was the Tuesday after the Sunday of It. Meredith was in the teachers' lounge drinking coffee and trying to smoke a cigarette. She'd never been very good at smoking. She thought she was holding it together pretty well, all things considered. She wasn't weeping uncontrollably, that was a start.

"Hey, English lady, you don't look so hot," Janey had said, flashing a crudely rolled joint in the palm of her hand and then making it disappear." Neat trick, huh? Why don't we go for a walk?"

They ended up taking the rest of the afternoon off. As they walked by the river smoking Janey's very bad pot, Meredith told Janey all about what had brought her to Calgary.

Not what . . . who.

Dirkland.

They'd met in Montreal. She was doing her doctorate in English and he was doing a Master's in Environmental Studies . . . not that any of that mattered. They never talked about either subject. They lived entirely in the shared moment. All they talked about was each other. The only people they talked to were each other and the only tense they knew was the present. They didn't discuss her boring childhood in boring London, Ontario. She never asked him about his past, what he'd done those three times he'd had to fly back home on family business. They never discussed their not discussing it. Meredith can't remember what she did during the weeks he was away. She did her work, she supposed, she lived her life. Those stretches of time are blurs in her mind, absences in her core.

The odd thing was that Dirkland wasn't really her type. Not that she was sure she had a type. Being the daughter of a Western University Business Administration professor, a man who understood the value of the faculty tuition discount, she had been obliged to do her undergraduate degree two blocks from where she'd grown up. She hadn't liked either type available — the hard-drinking macho-jock jerks or, as Janey put it, "the guys who you're not sure if they're gay or just from certain parts of southern Ontario."

At Cornell she'd flirted with lesbianism, but only theoretically and based largely on her obsessive rereading of Adrienne Rich's love poems. She'd gone to a reading and had wanted to give herself over to the poetess . . . but realized what a ludicrous notion it was on her way up to the podium. Her lesbianism passed and in retrospect it doesn't seem real.

By the time she came to McGill to do her Ph.D., a twenty-seven-year-old semi-virgin, semi because she had never felt anything and had only been penetrated three times, amounting to less than an hour of coitus, she was pretty sure she had the whole thing sorted out. What she wanted wasn't type A or B from her youth or another woman, but a man with a real intellect who was soulful and gentle, an artist. Even the dark side of this sort of man intrigued her. She wanted an effete, sober Bukowski.

Montreal seemed a promising place to find her dark poet. Instead, she found herself hanging around with what Janey called, "the bowl-heads . . . you know those guys with little bowl-haircuts who sit around drinking coffee and talking about *other* people's movies." Meredith dated a couple of them, slept with one, but still felt nothing.

Then, out of nowhere, there was Dirkland.

He was exactly what her father had said he would be. "All you little English Lit girls are looking for your Heathcliffs. Jane Austin and those awful Brontes put ridiculous expectations in your heads. The problem is that once you find your dashing captain, you'll lose all perspective. You'll see. It'll happen. My rational little girl will be swept away."

She knew the sort of girl he was talking about, but she was too good-looking to slide into that category of unnoticed bookworms, those mistresses of unrequited love she'd seen eagerly taking notes in seminars. Meredith could see how she might be mistaken for this sort, but, unlike most of them, she did get noticed by men, the As and the Bs and many more further down the alphabet. She had just never been ignited by one until Dirkland. Besides, she was no fan of the Victorian novel. "Well-written period Harlequins," was her usual missive. Part of it was just a rebellion against her father's stereotyping, but mostly, she wanted love on all planes — sexual, spiritual and especially intellectual. She wanted to understand love and she just didn't believe it was anything like what those 19th-century novelists described, where there was always a catch, a failing, a tragic element Meredith saw no place for.

Within a week of their meeting, Dirkland had moved into her apartment. No one said anything. It just was. Every night they lay together in a nest of blankets and read with their legs intertwined. When she went to sleep, he was there, his shoulder beneath her head. When she dreamed, he was there. He still is.

"Look, you got a hit." Janey punched her in the arm.

"I've got three."

"Check out bachelor number two. He sent a photo."

Meredith clicked on the mail from NORM_787. "Dear DONE_AWAY," it began.

"Screw the letter, show me the photo!" Janey screamed à la *Jerry McGuire*. NORM_787 was not bald, but balding rapidly. "You can tell, look at his droopy eyes and moustache. Once the face starts to fall, the hair has no choice but to follow."

Meredith closed NORM_787 and checked out her other suitors. Bachelors one and three wanted to know about the Faye Dunaway line. Was it her face, her legs or the whole package that most resembled the actress? And in what movie? These guys didn't even have the class to try to veil their vulgarity; they came right out with it.

"I knew it was a mistake to put that in."

"You needed a hook. Lonely bookworm doesn't cut it. Here, give me that," Janey said. She reached across Meredith for the mouse. "There's supposed to be over a thousand guys with ads on this thing. Let's check them out."

Meredith slid her chair over to the right, allowing Janey to take over at the computer.

Janey burped and blew her vodka breath past Meredith's nose.

"Excuse my French," she said.

Typical Janey.

"If my friends back home knew that I was a French teacher, they'd shit themselves. I can barely order soup in French, but this is Calgary, so where am I going to order soup in French?" Janey had said, that first day as they walked along the Bow. Janey explained that she'd grown up in Hudson, not Montreal.

"Hudson was hard-core English when I was a kid. Personally, I don't give a fuck. As for my name, LeBeau, it came from some Haitian guy I married so he could stay in the country. His buddies were supposed to give me two grand, but they only came up with about eight hundred. Fucking pricks. They totally gave me the creeps. But talk about not understanding a word these guys said in either language . . . Anyways, I never slept with the guy because he had some gross rash on his neck. Years later

I heard a rumor that he had AIDS. More like started the rumor, which is the point. The point is that sometimes when you don't have a clue what you're doing, but you have to step in and do something you are ultimately unprepared for, you can still end up taking over.

"That didn't come out quite right but you get the jism of it. Why do you take over? Because it's there and it can be you. I come to Calgary, bullshit my way into a job teaching French. A language I don't speak. I become the union rep so they can't fire my ass. Which they wouldn't anyhow, because I scare the shit out of them. So there you go."

"How can you bullshit your way into a job teaching French?" Meredith soon regretted asking.

"I sucked Hendrick's dick . . . barely. The whole thing lasted less than twenty seconds. He couldn't get it up. I let it flop on to his thigh and shot him a look of kiss-ass superior contempt. He gestures that he can get it up, but he's desperate, hopeless. So I laugh once and real cruel. His little thing turtles. It's all over. He's been in my pocket ever since. He can't look me in the eye. I own his ass. That's what I'm talking about."

Meredith is never sure when Janey is embellishing or outright lying. She said everything with this odd combination of humour and guttural frankness. Her eyes were always looking right into yours and they never gave anything away.

Janey took Meredith to a series of cowboy bars that night. Janey had a thing for cowboys. That's why she was in Calgary. Cowboys and horses. The face Janey made when she said the word "horses" was, in Meredith's opinion, overtly lascivious. The way she said "horse " was relatively inoffensive, since half the time she meant heroin. The plural form made all the difference. It gave rise to some nasty speculations as to the meaning of that certain glint that came into Janey's eye when she said or heard the word "Stampede."

Meredith spent the next three weeks following Janey to countless country/western bars. Janey spent her nights outrageously line-dancing, flirting with every steel-jawed man in sight and doing god knows what else with them when she disappeared for those 15-20-minute interludes. Meredith passed her time brooding over endless scotch and waters, avoiding all eye contact and wishing other people weren't around. She lost count of the number of drinks she polished off mulling over her relationship with Dirkland; that last time he'd come to her Calgary apartment . . . the last and the first. After making love they'd nested in her comforter.

"I can't come back," he had said. "I can't see you again. I love you too much."

On the twenty-first night Janey finally said, "Why don't you and me blow this shit-sickle stand and have an old fashion girly-girl walk and talk all the way home."

They walked the full five kilometres to Meredith's apartment. It was cold, but Janey was too drunk, and Meredith was too drunk and angry to care.

"You know what I hate about this city?" Meredith began. "Beyond the lack of culture and literacy . . . yes literacy? My first day in front of my AP class I introduced myself not as Meredith, but Merry English, their new English teacher. I didn't expect all of them to have read *Lucky Jim* but one would think that the allusion to Merrie Olde would get something? Miss English the English teacher should get a little rise, shouldn't it? And these are the AP kids!"

"That's what enrages you, that your students are stupid? Welcome to the real world." Janey pulled her sleeve and laughed.

"I should be teaching at some quaint New England college or translating some up-and-coming European poet, or be on the editorial board of some scholarly journal . . . That's the Real World. This place isn't the real world. In this place everyone wants to drive someplace where you can see the mountains. We never actually go to the mountains. Oh no, we could never do that, we just go to where we can see them."

"So fine, we'll go to the mountains."

"No, don't you see, I hate the mountains. They frighten me. And quite frankly I'm pissed off with you, Janey. You keep dragging me to these terrible places with awful men trying to . . . and I can't . . . and all I can do is think about . . . him . . . and you just don't give a shit, do you?"

"It's about time you got pissed off with me. I've been waiting for this. I thought you'd break by the third night."

"What are you talking about?"

"Look, you need a reality check. You need someone to focus your anger on. I never had a doubt it would be me."

"Janey . . ."

"That's what friends are for?"

"Are we friends?"

"Not until we kiss and make up."

Janey kissed her lightly on the lips. Meredith thought for a second that Janey was going to take it further, but Janey just laughed.

"C'mon, were almost home."

"Dirkland said that I wouldn't like it here and he was right," Meredith sighed.

"Dirkland," Janey said. "Now we're getting to the heart of it."

Meredith didn't get to the heart of it, not really. When they got back to her apartment, she told Janey what he had told her: That his father had died and Dirkland had to take over the family farm. It also meant he had to marry Stephie, the daughter of his father's partner. He had tried to get his younger brother to do it, but it was pointless because Stephie wanted *him*. Stephie generally got what Stephie wanted. She told Janey about going up to Dirkland's house, but she stopped there and began to back-track.

"I can't really blame him. Moving out here was my idea. I didn't even tell him I had applied to teach at Manning High. Until the acceptance let-ter came, I had completely blocked it out of my mind and then when it came, I just packed my bags and headed out here. It was crazy . . . stupid. When I got here and called him, he was so different . . ." she couldn't go on.

Meredith had expected Janey to say something, tell her how all men are pigs who compartmentalize, and that their feelings aren't real, or, if they are, those aren't the ones they show you. She'd expected Janey to say *something*, but she didn't. Janey took a beer out of her little knapsack and twisted the top off. Meredith cried into Janey's shoulder for the rest of the night. Janey patted her back and silently drank her beer with her free hand.

"Check this guy out," Janey said, pointing at the screen. "Thomas Crown looking for an affair."

Meredith focused in on the screen. "I don't think . . ."

"It doesn't mean he's married. It just means he looks like Steve McQueen, or maybe whoever the hell played him in the remake. Alec Baldwin? No, that was *The Getaway*. Anyways, movie-star looks."

"Janey, did you ever notice how disturbed most of the characters Faye Dunaway plays are? The whole sister/daughter breakdown in *Chinatown*, shooting up banks in *Bonnie and Clyde*, the way she makes love like a man in *Network*?"

"She's crazy, sure, but smart and tough. She's always smart and tough."

"I want to be tough and smart."

"You're the smartest person I know, Dr. English."

"Two days before I met you . . . 'the day you rescued' me, I call it, I drove out to Dirkland's house. I don't know why I did it, what possessed me, gave me the courage. When he said that we must never see each other again . . . so that day, I pretended I was doing a survey."

"A land survey?"

"No, a consumer survey. I bought a clipboard and wrote down some stupid questions in case Stephie answered the door. I planned it out the night before. It was so stupid. By the time I got to his door I was completely frozen. It was like I had been in a trance and snapped out of it when I heard the door open . . . I just had to see him again, just one more time. Do you see?"

Meredith hesitated. Janey put her bottle down and edged forward in her chair.

"The thing is . . ." Meredith couldn't go on. She turned her head away towards the window.

"Don't tell me," Janey finally said, "he was married all along. How many kids?"

"How did you know?"

"How did you not know?"

"He has two children," Meredith sighed and turned back towards Janey. "They are so beautiful. The little boy looks just like him. Dirkland answered the door . . . the way he could pretend that I, that we never existed. I was nobody. I was nothing to him. Dirkland . . ."

"Dickhead is more like it. Have some vodka."

"Her name isn't even Stephie, it's Christine . . ."

"Check it out," Janey said, swivelling in her chair. "You got a hit from the Thomas Crown guy. 'Dear DONE_AWAY,'" Janey read in a funny masculine voice. "'I too am a prolific reader and enjoy cocooning with my beloved . . .' blah blah blah . . . 'I have a post-graduate degree . . .' oooh, he likes horseback riding. If you don't want him . . . know what I'm saying? Here we go, he sent a picture . . . I'll ride that pony . . ."

Meredith couldn't hear Janey anymore. The whole world was becoming a blur. Her gaze drifted again to her window. Beyond her own blurred reflection, with its sanguine eyes and widow's peak, the Rocky Mountains loomed.

Meredith vaguely wondered how Faye Dunaway would play this scene.

TESLA'S DEATH MASK

*I*t's one of those rare times when the TV is on but the sound is off. There're chicks in the room. That explains it. Buddy wields the universal remote like a samurai, switching the audio over to the spirit of rock and roll and leaving the image on the TV. I make some crack about how Buddy's got to sheath his weapon. One chick, the one who's found herself next to me on the couch, nibbles, kind of . . . at least that's what I'm telling myself. I get a momentary jolt of self-satisfaction. I was good enough to get her engaged, talking to me. She says she's a singer, or wants to be, and goes on about some never-to-be crap concerning a recording session. She's wearing those low-rider jeans they're all wearing now. She doesn't have much of a tattoo on the small of her back. A single black rose on the right side, barely noticeable. Not like some of them. It turns out that we both work in shit-hole restaurants. I'm just starting to bitch about mine . . .

"You're way too good for that place," Buddy cuts me off. Classic Buddy being Buddy . . . which is probably good for me in the long run. He'd been holding his end with the other girl but he has the will to own the whole room. At this point we could try to interject, I guess, or try to continue on our own, but the subject remains Buddy's purview. The room belongs to him. All we can do is conspire in glances and eventual side-whispers. False intimacy at its best.

I lose interest in the stale thread of Buddy's oft-heard conversation and let my eyes wander. They are running a bio of Tesla on the History Channel. I don't know as much about him as I should. I should know everything. That's my function. I do know he competed with Edison and won, sort of, and I know there is a thing called the Tesla coil and we wouldn't have electricity without it. Not that I fully understand what the Tesla coil has to do with electricity, demonstrating once again that I don't fully understand a primal force in our universe . . . not that any of us in the room does, not really, at an instinctive level . . . certainly not like Tesla did. Buddy also wanted to watch the Tesla bio (because of the death-ray), but gave it up for the possibility of chicks.

Before the chicks turned up, before the Tesla bio started, it was just another night — me on my couch, Buddy splayed across his. We were watching *Playboy* magazine's 50th anniversary special on the dope-dealer-sized TV. I drifted in and out, imagining myself as a young Jimmy Caan in a Sonny Corleone suit hanging out in the Grotto playing pinball. Buddy, who's something of a Buddhist in a Bodi Dharma/shoa-lin kick-ass kind of way, wondered out loud what bitchin' karma you've got to have to end up with Hef's life. On screen Hef is grinning like an altzy old man remembering some ancient and forgotten secret.

"Think of the tonnage of titty he's tested for authenticity," I said to be funny. That's what I do. That's what I'm here for. Also, I wanted to get Buddy to flip the channel. There's only so much of someone else's good karma you can let stare you in the face. It takes less then four minutes for me to want Hef to come back in his next life as a common slug or krill . . . some kind of a bug I can stomp on.

The girl next to me, the nibbler, the one who is or wants to be a singer, turns from the primary chat, the one where Buddy holds the floor, and talks to me.

"I used to like this song . . ."

"How does that happen?" I startle her. It comes out harsh, not rude, too stammered to be rude, but definitely not the way I wanted it to come out. "You like something, it means something to you, then, gradually, sometimes for no reason at all, it's turned in you. Gone sour so you can taste it."

"Yes."

"Then you try to track down why the meaning changed. Sometimes it's obvious, like food that made you sick, or that overproof white rum that made me spend a day and a half in the bathtub. But a song or a painting, that's more personal, more complicated."

"I know what you mean," she says. And we have our first spark. Or so I'm thinking, so I'm telling myself. I'm about to ask what made her lose her love for the song, willing that glint into my eye, but Buddy is telling me to twist another joint for the girls. I do. What choice do I have? That's what I'm here for.

"Balance of the body is necessary in any sport, but it can only be reached through balance of the mind," Buddy pronounces. I think they're talking about skiing. So I pick up the green Bic, the one taped to the table because if it ain't tied down I'm going to steal it, and I spark the joint. I'm thinking of passing to the nibbler first, but it's Buddy's dope and he's a bit of a stickler. No point anyways. The song is over. The song is lost and my little singer has been swept back into the main flow of conversation, the magnet that is Buddy.

I sulk back into the silenced television. Nikolai Tesla is shown in an old black-and-white photo at Niagara Falls. He is looking over his plans for the hydroelectric plant that would light New York, put America on the industrial fast track and eventually lead to Love Canal. The singer breaks free from Buddy's pull. She seems to be smiling at me.

"I never listen to the radio," I say, apropos of nothing more than the sound of the DJ's voice getting under my skin.

"I listen all day at work," she gleams.

"I like to choose my own music." I press on, "I just can't stand all that DJ shtick."

"They don't choose the music . . ."

"I know, the program director does or at least draws up the play list. The point is, I like to be my own program director."

"I see what you mean."

Miraculously she's still smiling, both lips and eyes. Am I supposed to keep going along on this ridiculous current? Maybe I can connect the dots in some clever way, bring back the earlier theme of loss and rot. Do it smooth, like I meant it all along. Nothing seems to be coming. Luckily, I'm saved by the Buddy.

"So what did you girls do today?" he rings out with forceful inclusiveness.

"We went shopping," they squeal in giddy unison. My attention returns to Tesla. He is suing Marconi for patent violations. The image on screen changes to an illustration of a frightening tower irradiating lightening. The caption underneath reads "Worldwide Wireless Communication." Next, there is a photo of a man I think I recognize as J.P. Morgan. I may be wrong, but I'm pretty sure I've seen the same shot of him . . . probably on PBS, courtesy of the Ken Burns treasure chest.

"Why don't you twist another?" Buddy tosses a little baggy at me. The chick over by him is still smoking the last one, tipping the ash, wrongly gauging there to be enough left to pass over to the singer. Between them they manage to drop the joint twice. Eventually the singer guides what's left of it into one of the ashtrays. I can't watch this ugly ballet. I should keep my eyes down, my mouth shut and my fingers busy. But part of me is thinking that it's already over, me and the singer, that is. If she can't take the joint pass, how can she possibly live up to my standards? Besides, if I were going to fall in love with her, it already would have happened. That's the way it is. That's the way I am.

"I think the death-ray is coming up," I offer, as Buddy hits a rare lull in his ongoing monologue. He changes channels on the amp and the room is engrossed in Tesla's death-ray. It turns out I was right; it was J.P. Morgan in the photo. Tesla took Morgan's money, promising to create a wireless radio network, and tried to build his death-ray instead. When he fessed up, Morgan pulled the plug and invested in Marconi.

"He built it later," Buddy states as a fact and switches back over to the radio. The spirit of rock and roll is playing *Hello* by Lionel Ritchie. I look at the singer out of the corner of my eye and wonder if it's me she's looking for . . . and vice-versa, of course. Then I think about the girl I met last week. She's kind of cute, but doesn't like old movies. Bogart in particular. So, that was it for her. I took her number and never called.

"You should show them what you bought." It's the other chick and she's talking to the singer. The singer goes tomato red and I lose the semi-eye contact I thought we'd established, even if it was only based on a common antipathy for Lionel Ritchie.

"I really don't . . ."

"C'mon!"

"No!"

"Pleeeease." That's Buddy.

"Wellllll . . ."

"PLEEEEASE . . ." Me this time.

"Alright! Lingerie. I bought lingerie."

Dead silence.

Even the spirit of rock and roll has nothing to say.

"I have this weekend planned with . . . a friend who . . . with a friend and I wanted something special. I'm not the sort of woman who regularly shops for . . . well, you know, lingerie . . ."

She's going on about the time-share condo she's rented, the Jacuzzi she calls *un bain turbillon*, because it isn't a brand name in French, but a description and I'm staring at the TV thinking how it's all Tesla's fault. It's old Nikola's fault that there is a TV and a stereo, Jacuzzis and electromagnetic coils . . . in short, the whole modern world that moves at this terrible, dizzying speed. And he would not share the Nobel Prize with Edison. I look back at the singer and think maybe I was wrong, maybe love isn't spontaneous but can be generated, not by time-shares or *les bains turbillons,* but by some other invention . . . if only I could discover the secret of that coil.

Despite Buddy's urging, the singer will not model the new teddy for us. She looks to me to change the subject and set her free. I am momentarily lost in our old false intimacy, but quickly come to my senses and point to the screen. After all, that's what I'm here for.

The final frame of the biography is an iron cast of the father of modernity's face with the cold caption "Tesla's Death Mask" written underneath.

FAT BLONDE CHICKS

*F*at blonde chicks have always had a thing for me. You don't have to believe me. I usually don't believe it myself until it's too late, which is a big part of the problem. I can be so blind sometimes. Just ask Doris. Doris is the current FBC who has a thing for me. She doesn't believe me. She thinks I'm just trying to let her down easy. The thing is, I am. That doesn't mean it isn't true. She doesn't understand, or won't understand, or just likes to have temper tantrums. Take your pick. Here's what I try to give her by way of an explanation:

"You ever seen *Murder by Death*?"

"I think so," she says, looking puzzled.

"It's a Neil Simon detective spoof, with Peter Sellers, David Niven," I prompt. I go over the rest of the cast and plot. She nods along like she remembers but before I get close to the point . . .

"Jack, what's this got to do with what we were talking about? I was trying to tell you—"

"Peter Falk, who, like I said is doing the Bogey part, has this line: 'You ain't had a woman 'til you had a fat blondie waitress.'"

"That's very funny."

"He does a great drag on the 's,' and I always liked Peter Falk."

"So, I've been a waitress," she says with a hopeful smile. A smile I've seen on too many fat blonde faces.

"Stupid as this may sound, I made that line my motto, my mantra, my mission."

"Great!" The smile broadens.

"I find it more than a little weird, you know, in retrospect. The thing is, mission accomplished. Like, a long time ago. I'm all, you know . . . waitressed out. "

"Just how many waitresses have you had?" The smile teeters a bit. But she's still too hopeful.

"I used to keep a ledger. Let's just say it's a three-digit number and leave it at that."

Doris leaves in a bit of a huff. I'm not quite stupid enough to tell her a dramatic exit isn't all that convincing if your audience knows you're coming back with, "And another thing," in ten minutes.

She's pretending she doesn't approve of this kind of promiscuity. She kind of has to, I guess. I don't really approve of it either. She'll get over it. Only . . . only it's worse than she thinks.

Like I said before, I have the built-in advantage that fat blonde chicks have a thing for me. "You look like you could have been captain of the football team," dozens of them have told me. I wasn't. Not my game. As a kid I was a slacker, a bit of a rocker when I got off my ass. When I grew into a more ambitious kinda guy, I became what you might call a seasonal worker, a bit of a wanderer. I did some tree planting in the spring, tour guiding in the summer, fruit picking in the fall and I followed my thumb south most winters.

What I'm talking about here happened on the road during those long, hot winters. I had a strategy, you see. I used to ask truckers and salesmen, guys who would know, where the worst diners were and make a beeline for 'em. Not the best, you understand, the worst. Not only is there less competition, often no competition, but therein lie the lonely and the desperate, the heavy and the blonde. Back home in BC people were in pretty good shape, even then. The worst diners in the heart of the US of A on the other hand . . . talk about fat city. Most of the waitresses have got nothing to do because nobody eats there. They all wore nametags and had lonely eyes. It was just so easy, what with my dark-blue eyes and sculpted shoulders, combined with the appeal of the wise drifter. They never had a chance. It went right to the romantic in them. The wise part refers to the notebook I always carried for names and numbers, poems and pretensions. And I'm always reading something. I learned early on that you gotta have something to kill time on the road. Back then I read everyone from John LeCarré to James A. Michener.

I was quite the package for Lola, somewhere in Indiana who'd watched every other kid she graduated with get the hell out of town. I was a vision come true for any of the Ambers, Jills, Sandys and Janes whose stories, if not the same as Lola's, were pretty damn close. I never had to do much, just mention I was a-hitching and wasn't sure where I'd be a-staying.

"Start from the very beginning." Doris comes pounding back into my room wearing a gargantuan pink shower cap. "Keep it under 10 minutes."

"It's an ugly story."

It really is.

"I wasn't captain of anything in high school, but I was one of the cooler kids. As cool as you can be in Kamloops, BC, I guess. I had a regular girlfriend, Tina Shoen. She was a perky little brunette with sort of cat eyes and the only girl I'd gone all the way with, if you discount the hooker at my cousin's bachelor party and I did at the time because I was too drunk to remember it. Tina and I were real on-again, off-again, like you are when you're kids. So you can see my problem. I, in Peter Falk's opinion, hadn't had a woman yet. In waddles Louise. Louise Fencik. According to my sister, who'd been friends with her since the third grade, Louise always had a crush on me. I should have known by the way she couldn't talk when I was around. As you know, my natural inclination is to be sort of dense about this kind of thing."

"Like this morning?"

"I guess. So, I'm just coming back from a date/stupid fight with Tina. My mom's gone to my aunt's place outside of Penticton to hook up with some roadies they'd met touring with The Dead. My sister's at the store getting more beer, and tipsy Louise is all alone in our living room. I come in and start to bitch about my date. I don't think I even notice it's Louise on the couch instead of my mother or sister. I'm in the room, so she can't speak. She sort of gurgles. I see that look in her eyes, the one women get when they want you to kiss them. She had no way of knowing what was going to happen next. She may have been full of hope . . . but that's because she expected me to ignore her."

"You didn't though?" Doris draws back a little. She narrows her eyes. What's Doris thinking? The worst, probably. She's not far off. It could be argued I fulfilled Louise's deepest fantasy. It could also be argued I took advantage of both her crush on me and the fact she was drunk. That's my sister's take. Mine is much more severe.

"Do you want the play by play?" I ask, and Doris does. Her eyes tell me.

"I walked right up to her, still bitching about Tina, saying how lucky she was to have me. Louise didn't say anything, she just kept gurgling and staring. I start taking off her dress. I continue directing her hand to my incredible hard-on . . . do you really want me to continue?"

"I want all of it." Doris looks like she's getting turned on. She lets her kimono slide down her shoulder.

"We didn't go all the way. She was just starting to give me head when we heard my sister dragging her bicycle up onto the porch. I bolted. Not much more to tell. The thing is, Louise worked the counter at the golf course snack bar every summer. Maybe she wasn't a real waitress, technically speaking, but I had accomplished my Falkian goal. I had now slept with a woman. Except she was only 15 years old."

"I've got to check this." Doris rolls her eyes up. "But, we're not finished."

She gives me a long hard look.

Is that it? Her eyes want to know.

It isn't.

Besides my sister being pissed at me for weeks and Louise never coming around any more and looking shattered those times I did see her around town, which wasn't very often . . . The thing is she was more than just starting to give me head and I never touched her dress. What did I care? I just walked right up to her and took it out. I put it right in her face. I took two handfuls of her long, straight blonde hair. Holding on pretty tight I started bucking my hips. The sound of my sister jangling beer bottles and locking up her bike on the porch didn't slow me down. I came in Louise's mouth like an angry 17-year-old, which, of course, is exactly what I was.

I broke up with Tina for good and didn't . . . couldn't even think of sex for nearly six months. I thought everyone could see the rape on me, because that's what it was. I couldn't look a woman in the eye. The guilt wore away a bit by summer and my guard was down when I met Meg.

"I had a dog named Meg." Doris appears with an elaborately wrapped towel on her head. Her robe is casually falling open again.

"I was a tour guide out of Jasper. We were doing a three-week intensive nature hike. I was the number two guide, so I hung back with the slow pokes."

"Meg?"

"Exactly. We lag behind a bit. I'm trying to get her to catch up but she keeps going slower. I'm too thick to see this as the ploy it is, or might be. This goes on for two or three days before we make camp. By this time, a social order is beginning to set in. The happy campers are pairing off. What do I care? I'm getting paid to be there and as far as sex was concerned, I was on the wagon. When it's not raining, I like to sleep outside. No tent. No lean-to. Just the stars above. I found myself a little spot a bit removed from the campsite, just close enough to keep an eye on the others. On the second night Meg, mustering all her courage, comes out to where I'm sleeping and offers herself to me."

"What did she say?"

"How she'd fallen in love with me in the short time she'd known me. How she was putting it all on the line, coming to me like this. My first impulse was, well, let's say, to do what comes natural. I was still only 18. It didn't take much to get me excited."

"Who interrupted you this time?"

"No interruption needed. I told her I was surprised and flattered, but not interested. I'd learned impulse control. Well, that's what I told myself."

"I was hoping for something a little more racy," Doris says, running her tongue around the corner of her lips.

"So was she. So was everybody, apparently. For the rest of the trip, they all gave me a hard time, made a show of showing Meg sympathy. I thought I was doing the right thing, not taking advantage. Whatever. The point is, I was the only one who couldn't see Meg coming. That's the lesson. I wouldn't learn that one for . . . well, I probably haven't learned it yet. For a week after we got back to the base camp, people I didn't know gave me the cold shoulder, called me a prick under their breath when they walked by. I never worked out of Jasper again."

"You poor dear. Well, this has been illuminating." Doris actually closes my door softly on her way out.

Maybe she's giving up. I don't know. Doris took that better than I thought. The thing you gotta understand is what Meg said about putting it all on the line is almost exactly what Doris said to me this morning. That's what got this whole thing started: Doris hovering outside my room chain smoking. Me smelling the smoke and not sensing her there. When I opened the door I was surprised to see her.

I said: "Didn't you quit smoking?"

Then I noticed she had that look in her eye, like Louise and Meg and all the ones whose names I burned away; the barely perceptible quiver, the unblinking fear. She came right into my room, sat on my bed, looked up at me with those doughy FBC eyes and . . . declared? Is that the right word?

I thought I'd nipped it in the bud.

I said: "It's not real. It'll pass. You just have a thing for me because you're a fat blonde chick. It happens all the time. It's a long story. Can I just leave it at that for now?"

She said: "What the hell are you talking about?"

I said: "Can I go to the bathroom first?"

She said: "Are you going anywhere today?"

I said: "Do you want me out of the house?"

She said: "Just be quick about your business in the bathroom, will ya? Did you call me fat?"

I guess all those saids should be asks. Doris and I do that sometimes, kinda slip into playing at questions. When she comes back and she will be back, she's going to ask the $64 K question: "What the hell does any of this have to do with Peter Falk?" And I'm going to have to tell her about Barb Simons. She was older, old enough to be my buddy Chuck's mother, in fact. She also worked every breakfast shift at the King Eddy back in Kamloops. She's the one all the others are based on . . . the proto-fat blondie waitress. The way she smiled when she poured the coffee, rubbed her feet at the end of a shift, kept all the orders straight in her head . . .

Barb's the one Doris most reminds me of, in as much as they all haven't become one humongous blonde blur. With Doris it's different. They have the same body type, of course, but it's more of a personality thing. They're both funny, but that's a pretty common trait for FBCs. Maybe it's that they're funny in the same kind of way. Barb had two kinds of funny. There was the hardy-har-har kind for the customers and the clever inside stuff just for me. Either way, her trick was to make you, me, the customer — whoever was in front of her — feel kind of complicit with her. She's always letting you know you're in the know, whether it's that they got a new busboy who's a little lost, or telling me exactly what I'm thinking when I smile. You're in it with her and it's all just a little game for the two of you.

Sex with Barb was like that, too. She taught me how to please a woman, that's for sure. The whole thing became a question of rendering service with efficiency and grace. I'm not sure if this is a waitress thing, a fat thing, or a blonde thing, but Barb had it in spades. I try to picture Doris in her place, instructing me to the niceties of her body like she's recommending the daily special. It's still not there for me.

"So are you going to tell me what any of this has to do with fat blondie waitresses?" Doris is back again, now fully draped in towels.

"After I'd been on the road for a few years I asked a fellow-traveller, kind of reflectively, why it is that guys like waitresses so much. 'Because they serve us,' he said, like I'm some kind of an idiot."

"It does seem pretty obvious. But, you're such a self-service kind of guy. How many cups of coffee have I offered you? How many have you actually had?"

"I guess I'm going to have to tell you about the woman who made a man out of me."

"Now we're getting to the juicy stuff." She sits on my bed, making it wet. "She's the one I remind you of, right?

"Sort of, she's the one who started the whole thing off, my obsession with . . . you know, waitresses. The thing is she was a buddy's mother."

"And you did her? You bastard! How many times?"

"I'd rather not get graphic, you know, out of respect. I used to come around the King Eddy just after they stopped serving. We'd go back into the kitchen and she'd make me some eggs. Hell of a lot better than breakfast at home, which was usually potato chips and Diet Coke."

"I bet you two cooked up more than eggs."

"Bacon, sausages, you name it."

"Tell me about the sausage."

"Doris . . ."

"Tell me about the sausage. Pleeeeeeease tell me!" She leans back, making my pillow wet.

"Chuckie, that's my buddy, he found out and I couldn't show my face in town for months. The lesson I got from this one . . ."

"If she was an older woman she probably gave you a bunch of lessons. Why don't you tell me about one of them? Please, just a tiny piccolo. " She catches herself and snorts out a laugh. "I mean peccadillo. I did not mean that you have a small piccolo, sausage, whatever. You don't, do you?"

"Would it matter if I did?"

I look at her and see way too much thigh and beyond. She has that look in her eye again, but she's more confident. Has she always had that look in her eye for me or did she first get it this morning? I should ask her about that.

"Once I was out of town, things just seemed to fall into place. I hid out for a couple of days with my aunt in Penticton. Then I caught a ride to Boise. My plan was to hitch through Idaho to Oregon and maybe Northern California, get some work picking, construction . . . something was bound to turn up."

"So, who turned up?" Doris rolls her eyes.

"Stella Patterson of Missoula, Idaho."

"What's Stella's story?"

"She fell for me hard and fast. I didn't see it coming. My aunt's friend, the guy who said he'd take me to Boise, was in the bathroom when she brought the bill. This guy was always in the john when the bill came. Know the type?"

"My whole family. Once in a Chinese place, when the waiter came with the bill my whole family, like seven of us, were in the can. They almost called the cops."

"Stella wrote me a poem on the back of the bill."

"No fucking way. Do you remember it?"

"Christ no. Wait, maybe Missoula is in Washington."

"Very funny. You must have it somewhere."

"I don't keep mementos anymore."

"You're an odd fish, Jack. I'll give you that."

"She was the kind of girl who stayed up late at night naughtily reading romance novels. She was overly polite to her very few customers, cried when her boss screamed at her, and writing that poem to me was the single bravest act of her life. As a reward, I leeched off of her until the coast was clear, then headed back home."

"Why'd they let you show your face back in Kamloops?"

"Turns out Barb was also doing it with all of Chuckie's friends and he knew about at least two of them, so he couldn't really hold a grudge against me. The four of us, me, Chuckie and the other two guys got together and had a real drunk-up when I got back to town."

Doris doesn't seem to like the turn the conversation is taking. She crinkles her nose up and really reminds me of Barb. They're the same age. Doris is now how old Barb was then. The difference is I'm that age too, now. And here we are carrying on like kids. I'm about to bring this up . . .

"I just don't get you," Doris sighs. "I'm going to dry off."

What doesn't she get? She seems to like the sexy bits, but she isn't taking in the over-all message. I told her I leeched off of Stella for months. Shouldn't that set off alarms? I'd told Stella I was on the run, accused of a crime I didn't commit. She loved it. I loved that she loved it. It was fun, you know sneaking around, always playing at taking precautions. I was real proud of myself. I was her dark knight and to me she was like Barb and Louise and Meg all rolled into one. I got bored, of course. Restless. I kept calling home, running up her long-distance bill, not keeping a low profile at all.

When I got back to BC, I had nothing to do. I had no job. I had no goals. After the Meg debacle, Barb was a good thing for me. She was understanding and motherly, but not like my mom, who back then was still a party girl. By the time I got around to thinking about Stella, I found myself staring guilt right in the face. I felt like an asshole for lying to her and slowly bleeding her little savings account dry.

I had to figure out a way to get what I wanted without the guilt, without fucking everything up with the girl, my friends, my family, her friends and family . . . the whole damn town.

"So this friend's mother started you down the waitress road and you liked your first pit stop? Is that it? Am I caught up?" Doris is in the huge pink shower cap again. This time she's got it wrapped tightly over a head full of curlers. She's also back in her kimono and on my bed.

"Look, I'm sorry if this conversation hasn't been what you were hoping for. I usually don't go on about myself like this."

"No kidding. I've never even heard you talk about the book you're reading."

"If only you'd asked about that."

"It all comes back to this Barb woman, doesn't it?"

"In the beginning? No doubt. Then it became something else, a pattern, a ritual, an obsession. Barb got lost in the mix. They all have. Listen, after Stella, I felt guilty. I mean I'd gone into this big romantic hero routine, I was playing a part for her and I thought I was, you know, a good guy. But only . . ."

"Until her phone bill comes?"

"Exactly. So what I did was lay down ground rules for myself."

"That sounds like a good idea."

"It all depends on what the rules are and how closely you follow them."

"So . . . what were yours and how close did you come?"

"I came up with four basic rules. Don't lie. Let them come to me. Don't take more than I'm due. Get out quick and painless as possible. I was actually pretty good with one and two. Three and four, I had some troubles."

"No doubt."

"Until I gave up on them all together."

"Didn't it get boring? Seducing all those women?"

"I didn't see it that way. That's what number two was for. They came to me. That was the beauty of the rules. I never saw it coming until the last second, or at least I told myself I didn't, which got harder and harder to do as the years went by. I had to keep it up, though. There seems to be something about my not noticing the attraction until the very last second that these women found charming."

I look at Doris. Now I'm getting through. She'd seen that look on my face this morning and I'd seen her reaction. I felt myself on the verge of the next step, the one that had been the root of my success. I held back that little smile, the eye contact, first touch . . . the melting. I felt myself deploying it and stopped short. You have to understand, it's been a long time since I've slipped.

"I see," is all she says.

"It was like with Barb, that first time. I didn't see it coming at all. She was standing there watching me eat my eggs. Next thing I know she's giving me that look. I smile and I see this relief and joy in her eyes."

"Did it ever occur to you, Jack, that you might just be taking advantage of women who are a little lower on the sexual totem pole than you?"

"There is that. I guess I just wanted to be a hustler and didn't want to admit it to myself."

Doris shakes her head. "I just can't imagine you hustling anyone, Jack."

"That's our whole problem here, Doris. I used to think I was just a guy with an affinity for a certain type of woman, or a guy a certain type of woman has an affinity for. I'm never really sure. I did let them come to me. I never directly hit on a waitress. I didn't even tip especially well. Most times I didn't even end up paying for my meal. That's always how it'd start, with the feeding. Once they've fed you, they're connected to you. Simple as that."

"That's why you don't drink my coffee?"

She's got that right. We sit and look at each other. I've got to end this.

"Doris, I sponged off of all these women and left while the leaving was good every time. I told them it was better to part while it was still a fling and not a relationship, fun but not forever and don't worry sweetheart, I'll be back, I'm just a creature of the four winds and have to blow . . . and I could still tell myself I was being a good boy."

"So, what are you now, Jack? Some kind of a monk?" Doris says, trying to make it sound like a joke. It doesn't come out that way.

"I've realized the error of my ways."

"Have you? For Chrissake, if this Barb woman were your mother, you'd kill your father just to marry her. Big news. You want a mommy replacement, big deal. It don't take Freud to figure it out. Look Jack, we're both grown-ups now and I don't intend to be your sugar momma."

"There's a little more to it than that. Her name was Shari. I only went out with her one time, but I'll always remember her because she wasn't a real blonde."

"So?"

Here it comes. Doris slides her elbows back and braces herself. I can see most of her breasts, including her right nipple.

"I was hooked up with this woman, Holly. She waitressed, but she also owned the joint. By this point I'd already gone from being the surprised innocent to a specialty gigolo. It wasn't about a Barb replacement anymore. I was in some bizarre holding pattern. I kept leaping from one fantasy cycle to the next. I knew I could live off of these women so why break my back picking fruit? Why live in the woods when I can spend my days in Holly's penthouse and become a personal ads junkie? I'm serious here, Doris. I looked for words like voluptuous and Queen-sized. If something bigger, better, and blonder than Holly came along, so be it."

"Look, I don't think you're hustling me, Jack, so you're not. I just want to make that perfectly clear."

"I don't think I am either, Doris, but that doesn't mean I'm not. Look, let me get back to Shari. I'd got her off the telephone dating service. The way she rushed when she said she weighed 145 lbs, I just knew. I think it was in Ann Arbor, Michigan. Maybe it was some other college town. I was a little older by then. Older than the college kids, I mean. I knew it as soon as I saw her walking into the student union building. She had that look in her eyes faster than I'd ever seen it. But it was different somehow. I only figured out why afterwards."

"After what?"

Our eyes connect and we're frozen in each other's headlights.

"After I sexually assaulted her." My heart stops.

"Like the first one, Louise."

"You caught that?"

We smile.

"She took me back to her place. She went to get some drinks and I asked to use her phone. Holly had been paging me all night. I called her back and we had a whispering fight . . . well I whispered. When I came back into the living room Shari was reclining on the couch. She let out this sort of gurgle and I just . . . ."

"You just what, Jack?"

"I just took my thing out and shoved it in her mouth. I grabbed her hair . . ."

"Oh, Jack."

"She didn't want to press charges. No need for that. She told me that what I had done, that . . . rape . . . was what she had been hoping for. I'd been fulfilling her fantasy. She told me that was the signal she was sending me. You see, by the time I got back she'd taken her panties off and had her legs open. She figured I'd see she wasn't a real blonde and my natural reaction would be to reject her genitals. That night I burned all my notebooks, left Holly, and left those parts of myself behind. I said good-bye to the hustler, the innocent and the rapist. I have never looked back. There's your totem pole."

This time Doris leaves for good. That's what I think. I might be wrong. I've been out of action for a long time now, since Shari, and my instincts aren't real strong to begin with. My life hasn't changed much. I'm still something of a wandering man. I spend most of the time on the road and in the bush, free and alone, serving my fat blonde penance. I still like to read, but choose from a wider range of authors, from Allende to Zola. I don't eat in diners so much anymore. When I do, I pay my bill, tip well enough not to be noticed and move on.

The thing is I like my little room over Doris's garage. I like fixing things up around the house. I even like Doris. Maybe I should just tell her that. Tell her we get along great being landlady and tenant. Tell her I'm happy to pay the rent and that I respect her too much . . . That'll never work, even if it is true. As I'm thinking all this, I'm already at her bedroom door. It opens before I have a chance to knock. Doris is wearing nothing at all.

"I dyed my hair auburn," she says.

"That's all I was asking," I say, and go in.

THE AGE OF IMPROV

*G*il slides out from the wings and drifts up the far aisle to the back of the house. He had been looking forward to this show all week and to the festival it was part of for months. *Billygoat Chew Toys* was *the* hot troupe right now. They had a pilot deal with ShowTime or HBO. They were staying at a bigger and better hotel than everyone else. Gil knew one of them, had met him at a closing-night party at some other festival a couple of years back . . . Mark, Max, Matt . . . an M-A name for sure. The guy was a total poseur. One of them, maybe M-A, maybe one of the others, was supposed to show for the first round of the Theatresports play-offs, but didn't make it into town on time. Backstage he had asked Randy, the venue manager, about it. Randy didn't know anything. Just as well; Gil really didn't want to dwell on the Theatresports.

They'd packed the house, you had to give them that. Gil settles himself into a seat in the back row beside an incredible blonde in a black tank top. His eyes nearly fell into her cleavage as he passed. Is she really with that nerdy-looking guy in the baseball cap? Gil shouldn't be thinking about these things, considering what it took to get him here.

He turns away from the killer blonde, closes his eyes and exhales deeply. His brilliant escape begins playing in the theatre of his mind.

"Do Gorillas fly? Of course I'm going," Gil sees himself saying. "They couldn't have it without me."

Kathy shoots him her death-ray look and keeps changing the baby with grim determination.

Never giving up eye contact, Gil keeps on, "C'mon Kath, I'll be gone a week, ten days tops. It's not like before when a tour could last forever."

He sees himself begging in character.

First, "Forever is never long enough. Pleeeeease," as the little boy he calls Philip. Then a quick, "What will it take to put me on that bus today?" as Ted Taylor, crackerjack car salesman.

Kathy isn't biting

He tries again as Weary O'Leary, Irish poet extraordinaire, and Inspector MacGrumble of Scotland Yard. No dice.

As a last resort Gil tries, "I only have eyes for one other woman, Kath, this little missy here," à la John Wayne. He picks up his daughter. "You'll miss your Daddy, won't you? You know your daddy won't be looking at other little babies, don't you?" Then to Kathy, "They're all kids at these things, you know that."

"Well, you're no kid."

Gil burps the baby. He gives Kathy his irresistible little smile. The one she said she fell in love with. The one she always tells him, "Makes you look like you've gotten away with murder." He zooms into to an extreme close-up of his smile and holds it for a long beat.

Cut to Kathy, mid-shot: "Fine, but if you're gone any longer than a week, I can't promise we'll still be here when you get back. And if I smell anything I don't like . . ."

"You hear that kid? We're going to Disneyland!"

He tosses his baby girl in the air and sees his own face from her point of view as she makes her descent into his long, hairy arms.

So far the festival had been a disappointment for Gil. None of these kids had the spark of the outlaw in them. It was all celebrity impersonation and one-joke bits no one knew how to end. There was nothing political. Nothing anywhere near the edge. One of the troupes from England had a pretty good sense of the surreal, but that's the Brits for you, kaka jokes out of left field and Bob's your uncle.

He opens his eyes and scans the crowd, coming to rest on the blonde beside him, like he knew he would. What a number this one is, if she was alone the whole trip might be worth it, but she is definitely with "Baseball-cap." She's all over him, bubbling over about *The Gophers*, some improv troupe from Wisconsin or North Dakota.

"They're so musical," she's saying, "they could, like make it in the recording industry if they wanted to. But they're, like, artists." She has her arm splayed across his chest, her mouth close enough to lick his ear.

Gil can't watch. Thinking about gophers, he closes his eyes again. He sees the troupe, not the varmint. What got *The Gophers* going? What separates them from all the other little rats? What's their story? They're probably just another nest of farm boys who happen to see the lighter side of bestiality. Five healthy young men in overalls behind a barn. One of them is grooming a horse. Gil senses his mind veering towards gay porn and steers clear. Forget the fucking *Gophers*, first-timer wannabes . . . unlike Gil. Gil has paid his dues.

No one wants to hear about it and Gil doesn't particularly want to talk to anyone about it . . . no one here at least. God, there's nothing more pathetic than those good old fucks who keep talking about the good old days. "I remember back in ought-six . . . ." There is a time and a place for war stories.

Gil flips channels on his mind screen and he sees himself chatting with Letterman.

They're not on the show; they're in Dave's big house in Connecticut. Gil and David Letterman are in Dave's plush living room. Dave lights a cigar and offers one to Gil.

"I've been a Gorilla fan for a long time." Letterman smiles meekly. "Gil. I can call you that, right?"

"I love your deadpan, Dave." Gil takes the proffered cigar.

"Seriously, I've always wondered about something," Dave says as he leans in. "Did you call it New Gorilla because you, yourself, look so much like an orangutan?"

"With my pants off, I'm more of a baboon. Bad joke, boy is my ass red. Seriously, it's a good story, I'm glad you asked. Let me ask you something, Dave. Do you remember Joe Cocker's first appearance on *Saturday Night Live* in '76 or '77? That's the night *New Gorilla Theatre* was formed. Picture the scene: 11:30 p.m., three little kids up way past their bedtime, sneaking down the backstairs to my parents' basement. The goal? To watch *SNL*, like we did, or tried to do every Saturday night."

Dave is making Dave faces.

Gil shifts in his chair, fumbles with the cigar. "Once we get by the guard dog and are safely in the basement, we can't even bring ourselves to touch the knob on the TV. We listen. No one moves until we are convinced our parents haven't heard us. The whole thing is like a secret mission, you know, when you're a kid you're always a commando with self-destructing orders."

Paul Shaffer and the band seem to have appeared and Gil feels like there's a live studio audience watching them.

Still relatively unperturbed, he continues, "That particular night, that incredible show where Cocker is singing "With a Little Help from My Friends" and John Belushi comes out and starts doing the best Cocker impersonation there can be. At first Cocker takes it okay, lets Belushi in. Tries to laugh it off. Then it starts to get to him. He tries to shoo him away, he's got 'back off mate' in his eyes." Gil looks over to make sure Dave is properly rapt. He isn't. He is playing with a cue card, lining it up with the others on the desk that has suddenly materialized in front of him. Paul Shaffer is waiting for his cue to cut in like a dog wanting a treat.

"Belushi doesn't stop. He starts doing Cocker better than Cocker. He's got him: the spastic movements, the contorted faces, the voice and affect right on the money." Gil can sense Paul's fingers over the first chord of "With a Little Help from My Friends." He speaks frantically. "Joe starts getting really pissed off, but Belushi just keeps right on going. This is it! Nothing is sacred! We all felt it. It was like a sacrilegious cpiphany? Is thcre a word for that?"

Dave's hand is in the air. His lip is curling. He looks over Gil's shoulder. Gil senses the producer back there, sliding his finger across his throat.

Gil hits full panic. Dave inhales and it's now or never, so Gil blurts out, "I was with Mickey Solomon!"

Dave smiles and they are in the Ed Sullivan Theater. Mickey Solomon, the great Mickey Solomon, one of Dave's faves, is back on the show and Gil isn't there at all anymore.

Gil doesn't get to tell how he, his sister Charlotte (the most talented of the three of them, hands down), and the great Mickey Solomon giggled all night long. How they knew from that day what their calling was. How they hung blankets from Gil's bed turning the lower bunk into a little stage.

Even in his daydream he can't tell Dave about the look in Mickey's eye when he came up with the name *New Gorilla Theatre*.

Something brushes Gil's arm. It's the blonde. She's taking off her tight little jean jacket. She smiles an apology. Gil want to smile back, but his eyes widen as "Baseball-cap" removes his namesake to reveal a very pasty bald pate. This guy is going bald and not good bald either — like Ron Howard bald — and Gil is momentarily horrified. The blonde turns the other way and the chance is lost.

Gil looks around, pretending to be cool. The house lights are still on. Most of the seats have been filled. Those not seated are looking for vacancies; a few have resigned themselves to sitting on the small staircases coming off the wings of the stage.

Gil closes his eyes again and tries to re-enter the theatre of his mind. He hears his inner voice tell the story of the morning the three of them first performed for Gil's parents. He tries to picture his mother asking if it was New Gorilla or New Guerilla Theatre, Mickey disappearing under the table, Charlotte sitting there with her crooked, funny smile . . . He wants to tell it to Dave, to the hot blonde, to someone . . . all he sees is the dull house lights playing red on the inside of his eyelids. He focuses on that light, lets his mind play with it until it becomes that famous photograph of Ché Guevara drawn on so as to make him look very much like a Gorilla. The company logo from the day Charlotte drew it and stuck it on a hat.

A montage of all the faces who've worn the pink beret flash by, leaving room for the next face with crooked haste: Mickey and Charlotte, of course, Sam and Terry who'd joined after high school and who both played guitar, Simon, Jill, who was more of a groupie, Billy Fahey, those two kids who Gil had gone to the Renaissance festival with and were never members, but he'd given them hats . . .

Gil wished he'd brought his pink Ché beret to the festival. He knew he'd feel like an idiot wearing it given the circumstances, being the only member of the company present. Still, it might help him get recognized, if not by this new lot of performers, at least by the general public. Back in the old days *New Gorilla* had played this festival like clockwork and done pretty well, filling the house when they had good time slots.

Gil can't believe his eyes. "Ron Howard Bald" is shooing the fabulous blonde off of himself so he can reach into his pocket for his cellular phone. The guy is actually taking a call in the theatre. Unbelievable. "Put a lid on it for a sec," the guy is saying in a sharp whisper to this woman he so obviously doesn't deserve. "I gotta take this call."

At least he puts his baseball cap back on before he gets up and heads for the exit, grunting into his phone, leaving Gil with the killer blonde. Gil wants to say something, but can't come up with a line. How can that be?

It's the opening-night party all over again.

It was a terrible night. He should have known it would be based on how incredibly young everyone there seemed to look and the awful, awful music they played. They all dressed new-wave hippy without any idea what it was supposed to mean. Nobody was talking shop. That's not true. They were talking shop, but only about the money and the possibility of celebrity gains. What it takes to make it. If they weren't talking about how they were going to make it, it was a story about someone else who had. Gil, being the great Mickey Solomon's best friend, had a doozey to tell, but sat on his tongue all night.

It wasn't like the old days, that's for sure. No one was doing any bits, telling tall tales, getting naked for the hell of it . . . none of the stuff that made these things what they were supposed to be — sexual survival of the most talented. In the old days, Mickey would make a point of scoring at every festival party he attended, even in that last year, that final all-out tour.

Gil had had his share, but Mickey was the master. He used that face he made in the organ-grinder skit and they fell like leaves before him.

Gil has no trouble conjuring the footage of that bit: Gil in the stupid hat, the droopy moustache that keeps falling off, Mickey in his stupider, little hat, his face that of a monkey. No makeup, just talent.

From the top: Gil singing "O Solo Mio," Mickey on the end of his chain, holding out a tin cup to the first row of the audience.

"Itsa no use," Gil moans. "Nobody a-wanna see my monkey no more!" Fast forward through Gil pouring his heart out to the crowd, Mickey monkeying it up, jumping into people's laps, kissing women and picking their pockets.

"Ah, but watta can I a-do, my little a-monkey-friend?" Gil finally sighs.

"Talk with a better Italian accent than that," Mickey snaps back through his monkey smile, that knowing primate grin on the backdrop of his fine, slight features that made all the girls swoon.

Gil goes berserk and chases Mickey around the stage. He gets angrier and angrier until he finally transforms into a big ape. As Gil starts loping about the stage, Mickey turns into Mussolini and starts giving a raucous fascist speech in Italian.

Gil goes nuts, pounding his chest. The crowd chants, "GIL-MORE! GIL-MORE!"

Gil does the trademark *New Gorilla* knuckle-walk off the stage and into the crowd. He beats his chest letting out big ape screams. He chooses a hot chick at random and slings her over his shoulder . . .

Gil elbows the fabulous blonde beside him.

She turns quickly, her big tits jiggling. Gil smiles sheepishly and points vaguely to the guy on the other side of him.

There's going to be no knuckle-walking here.

No Mickey either, of course, Mickey being so fucking big now. No Charlotte, her being so married to that dead boring dentist, Philip. No Sam or Terry or Bill or Stacy or any of the others who'd worn the pink beret. This year Sam couldn't get away from his job and Terrence . . . Terrence just said he didn't want to do it anymore. Gil didn't try to call any of the others.

It would have been nice to have one of them around at the opening-night party. Any of them. Gil tried to mingle. Introduced himself to a few people as "John Gilmore, you know, GIL-MORE! From *New Gorilla*?" He looked into their blank eyes and had to say, "Oh, we're not really here right now, but we've been around forever. Everyone calls me Gil." It was all he could do not to mention Mickey's name. By 10:30 he'd given himself up to a bottle of rye. He didn't even bother trying to latch onto a Theatresports Team, his ulterior/real motive in going to the party, now that he was a married man not trying to get laid. He'd just have to show up when the tournament started and feel his way around.

That's another story.

Gil turns to the blonde, still not sure what he's going to say, trusting his ability to go with whatever comes out of his mouth. "Mr. Really-needs-the-baseball-cap-and-cellular-phone" slimes back into the house just as the first note sounds in Gil's throat. The blonde, who's been avidly reading her program spins in her seat on hearing the door creak. Her heel catches Gil's bony knee. She quickly turns her head, giving a smiling apology. Gil tries to smile back. Too late, "Really Needs" is back in his seat and her hands are caressing his ears and her lips are at his pale neck whispering sweet anythings.

The theatre is bathed in darkness.

The crowd quiets. The blonde settles her head on "Really Needs'" chest. Gil focuses his full attention on the stage.

The curtain comes up to reveal a blank stage lit by five spotlights, making five interlocking circles of sharp white light on the black floor. The music from *Chariots of Fire* drifts in over the new sound system. This place is way better than it was the one time Gil got to play it. Someone had poured a truckload of money into it. Too bad no one thought to give any of the smaller venues any attention.

The crowd is dead silent now.

The music grows in intensity.

A donut rolls through the circles of light.

Everyone leans forward, straining to see what's going on, reacting to the motion like cats. Two more donuts roll across the stage, timed to the music, then two more. Gil senses what's coming.

A whole bunch more donuts spin in from the wings and the audience twitters.

A man in a bodysuit, complete with a 12" dildo stitched onto the crotch, waving his arm over his head and screaming like a wounded turkey, follows the next volley of donuts. The man leaps off stage right. He is followed by four more guys in bodysuits trying to fuck the non-stop flow of rolling donuts with their big dildos. Gil knew it, but is laughing along with the rest of the crowd. He glances at the blonde. She's loving it. "Really Needs" is rolling his eyes and looks like he's going to snort.

Gil looks back to the stage, the lights are panning from the floor to the backdrop, becoming the Olympic rings. A final row of donuts emanates from back stage directly towards the audience. The five members of *Billygoat Chew Toys* run full tilt towards the hysterical crowd in hot pursuit of the rolling donuts. Four of them leap right at the audience who have completely failed to form a mosh pit. The four *Billygoats* gyrate their way over the first four rows of startled heads before the hoists they are attached to reel them in.

"I can't tell you how many people have told us to take a flying fuck at a rolling donut over the years," says the fifth one, M-A. Gil recognizes him immediately. M-A had stayed put at the edge of the stage. "As you'll find out, ladies and gentlemen, we are the sort of people who take things very literally. We are *Billygoat Chew Toys*!"

The crowd goes nuts.

The hot chicks down at the front start chanting "CHEW TOYS! CHEW TOYS!" Gil is swept away for a moment, cheering for the Goats, flashing on the "GIL-MORE! GIL-MORE!" image he'd been in moments before.

The blonde is on her feet, bouncing up and down in a way no one could help but notice. "Really Needs" is getting another call. It isn't ringing at least, but Gil sees the thing vibrating in the side pocket of the guy's satin windbreaker. He takes the call and is out before the end of the flying fuck bit.

Gil thinks of following, but doesn't want to be rude to the Goats. He likes the way they get the crowd involved. M-A entices audience members to give other targets for the actors to take flying fucks at. They do a couple of good physical bits, but it drags. M-A is a bit grating, at least to Gil, smug like a young Tom Hanks. He has a good way out of the skit though . . .

"I realize it's early goings, folks, but we'd like to take our intermission now, you know, to sweep up the donuts. We gotta have something to serve tomorrow night's crowd."

This segues into a James Bond as a nanny skit, a sort of what he does between missions kind of thing. Gil's finding their stuff good, but a little too prop dependent. Gil could hardly complain, for the first two years *New Gorilla's* motto had been: "Always wear an ass-pad."

It's not about props. It's about people. How many characters had Gil played? A hundred? A thousand? A hundred thousand? Sure Mickey got nominated for an Emmy, but he's been playing the same character for six years. Where's the fun in that?

On stage, they were finally removing their goat prop to the wings and ending the skit. Give 'em credit, they're sticking to their take-everything-literally theme. Dirty though, the whole show so far, right in the gutter.

"Really Needs" gets back to his seat pretty quietly. The blonde makes a bit of a fuss at his return, but Gil doesn't really want to give her a piece of his mind about it. Gil gives the guy a closer look. He seems familiar. Was he at the thing last night? Had Gil actually watched this guy perform, maybe at Theatresports?

Theatresports.

Gil had failed to latch onto a team. He only knew a couple of the people involved, that one kid from *Hot 'n' Trots* and his girlfriend. Gil wasn't sure if she acted or just hung out. He didn't know anyone on the inside anymore; it had been three years since he'd been here. After being shuffled from one know-nothing volunteer to another, and finally to the venue manager who told him who the tournament coordinator was, it was way too late to join. Maybe out of pity, maybe because the *Hot 'n' Trots* or someone else said something, maybe both, the coordinator came back and asked him to be a judge.

"Who am I to judge?" Gil asked. The guy didn't get that it was meant rhetorically.

It had been a very long night.

Gil nodded off during one of the bits and the team on stage had integrated it into their groove. Gil couldn't blame them. It was the thing to do. He'd have done it himself.

By the time he'd dragged his sorry ass back to his hotel room it was too late to call Kathy. He didn't think he'd miss her or the kid or the conventional life they represented, but alone in that room, he did. Gil had stayed up thinking about going home until it was too late to catch the last bus.

The Billygoat Chew Toys are doing the organ-grinder skit.

Gil's organ-grinder skit. His and Mickey's.

M-A is playing Gil's part and getting it all wrong and their little guy has nothing on Mickey. How can this be happening? M-A had said that he'd never seen *New Gorilla* that time they'd talked way back when. Gil distinctly remembered that, it was probably why he didn't like the guy. The whole point of going to these festivals was to support fellow artists, foster a community. Even back when Gil met M-A, he and the rest of his troupe were staying at a better hotel and M-A whined about not wanting to see anyone else perform. Apparently someone had seen him and Mickey, if not M-A, one of the others. Gil's anger mounts. He scans the crowd looking for familiar faces, someone else who understands what's

going on, what these *Billygoat* thieves are up to. Gil tries to catch a
glimpse of Randy backstage. He's thinking of getting out of his goddamn
seat, crawling over the blonde and her insipid boyfriend and marching
right down to the stage to call these guys out.

Then two things happen:

"Really Needs" gets another call. This time the blonde hears it, or
rather she feels it vibrating against her ear, which is still pressed to his
chest; and the guy playing Mickey's part turns into Roberto Bennini,
instead of Benito Mussolini.

"Really Needs" and Gil both get up.

Gil wants to punch the man, rip his girlfriend's shirt off and scream
uncontrollably. Gil pauses. What he really wants to do is storm the stage,
strangle M-A, tell the goddamn paying public what these fucking bastards
are up to . . . But the Bennini is running through the audience hugging
people. The crowd is eating it up. They are embracing him.

Gil does not want to be embraced.

"Really Needs" heads straight for the exit, already murmuring to
whomever is on the other end. Gil follows him through the lobby and into
the street. Gil walks right up to him. He's got to say something to this guy
about manners, the sanctity of the theatre . . .

Surprisingly the guy recognizes Gil, he rolls his eyes with a complicit smile and silently offers a cigarette.

Gil takes the smoke.

The guy hands him a lighter, giving him the "I'll-be-off-in-a-minute"
finger and turns his back to finish his call.

"Sorry, I heard you. I was just giving a fellow victim a little relief,"
he says into his phone. "Cancel my 1:30 . . . yes and thank-you for saving me . . . You have no idea how painful it was . . . The things a grown
man has to put up with . . . Oh, she's sensational. Which reminds me; turn
the waitress part into a speaking role but nothing we can't cut out in post
. . . You don't believe me? When I went back after your last call, thanks
for that one too, by the way, they were trying to fellate each other with a
stuffed goat. I shit you not, a stuffed goat . . . No, a real goat they'd sent
off to the taxidermist . . . And these guys are supposed to be the cream of
the crop . . . You call that art? What's that saying? 'Anyone who isn't an
artist when he's twenty has no heart, anyone who's still an artist at thirty

has no brain.' . . . Artist, communist, same thing . . . Yeah, I guess, but one of them was doing a Bennini impersonation . . . Improv, my ass, once you've done this shit for a week it's all just being too lazy to remember your lines. . . OK, I'll chill . . . Like you say, they're kids, they'll grow out of it . . . No, I think I'll have another butt and commiserate with this other guy who left the show. You're the best."

Ralph Shulman, producer, director and star maker, presses the "End" button on his cellular phone. He turns to the guy with taste, the guy who'd left the show with an air of disgust he can appreciate. He's all set to offer him another cigarette, have a chat about the business maybe, the guy seemed to be good people. Ralph Shulman knows people. He makes them.

But the guy is gone.

AUTOMOTIVE

*Y*ou are dreaming that you are driving a car.

It's late at night and eerily quiet, but you don't seem to mind. You're on a road you know well, a major boulevard that links the neighbourhood you grew up in to the one where you now live. It's a road you've driven hundreds of times, thousands. It's the road you took going to school, the one you drive each day to work. At first, you don't know how you know that it's that particular street. You can't see any of the landmarks; the big gray-stone house with the circular driveway, the Gothic church, the little park where you first . . . they are phantoms of that warm darkness looming beyond the influence of the streetlamps.

Sight doesn't matter. You tell people you can drive this stretch blindfolded. If they dare you to, you will. You know this road by feel. You know its hills and contours, the subtle grain of the asphalt, the one unique to this road, the one that grips your tires almost lovingly. It is a texture to be found exclusively on the boulevard of your dream.

So, you're humming along. The one finger you use to steer, the right index, hooked on at the 6 o'clock position, acts as a conduit for your intimate connection to the road. With nothing but the broad, empty lanes in front of you, you speed up a little. Then a lot. It's not that you're in a hurry. You're not going anywhere. You know the lights will all be green at any speed. So you go faster and faster because you can, because you know the road like the back of your hand and can feel its pull beneath you, holding you in its centrifugal cradle.

Now you're coming to the best part.

The crest of that long, winding hill cuts your headlights off at the knees. You place your hand on top of the steering wheel in preparation for the prolonged left lean followed by the majestic, sweeping right. You shift into neutral and move your feet steadfastly away from the pedals. It's the sort of thing you did when you were sixteen to impress your friends when you were drunk with their company.

In the hanging moment before the descent, you slowly glance to your right. You had been completely alone, of that you had been sure; there is now a child in the seat beside you. You are not surprised. You smile your roller-coaster smile and receive a complicit wink in return. You reach into your pocket and remove a large handkerchief and present it to the child. The swatch of cotton changes hands and you let yourself be blindfolded.

As you feel the gathering momentum, that slight strain on the under-side of your arm as you hold the turn, it suddenly occurs to you the child is too young to be in the front seat. A toddler like that should be in the back, safely imprisoned in some death-proof contraption. You tug at the corner of the handkerchief, just to make sure, but the toddler has grown into a child proper and is now more noticeably you. You as you were on the way to school. You, when you were just beginning to understand your connection with this particular stretch of road, to feel an affinity towards other beings.

The child who is you smiles and the you as you are, who is driving, replaces the blindfold. The road, your will or some unfathomable con-spiracy of the two, begins to swing the steering wheel to the right. You've come to the snake in the road, you feel the pull through the soles of your feet. There is a silence to your screams, a first clear view of the boulevard, a freeze-frame snapshot in broad daylight of the dangerous intersection at the bottom of the hill. You see all of this on the inside of your eyelids. You're no longer sure that the light at the bottom of the hill will be green.

The snapshot disappears and darkness reigns. Yet, there is a building lightness within you, a weightlessness that comes from going though the dangerous intersection blindfolded, expecting the silence of screeching brakes, blaring horns and the awful whine of metal crumpling into metal.

It is late afternoon and you are almost home. The child in the passen-ger seat is not you, but your child. You know it is yours. Even though you've never seen this particular child before, it can be nothing but part of you. There is a certainty to your connection, a bond greater than the blindfold you hold between you. You effortlessly weave between the other cars; they are ghost ships driven by phantoms, blurs behind the wheel drifting in slow motion, politely giving way.

You've come to the stretch where all the houses look the same. There is a security in this repetition of split-level family homes, slanted driveways and perfect lawns. You feign confusion to amuse your child, be complicit in pretending not to know which house is home . . . but your child is no longer there.

The road disappears beneath you and you are in your bed, terrifyingly awake, hot with sweat. Your car is parked snugly in your driveway. The street is peaceful. The rest of the world still sleeps. And you know for a fact that someone you love has died.

COLLISIONS

*H*oward dresses himself as he does every morning; loose-fitting cotton pants with an elastic waistband around the back and a drawstring in front, white cotton socks and a bright poly/cotton short-sleeve monochrome shirt with the top button done up. Today Howard's shirt is banana yellow; his pants this week are beige. He had polished his brown penny-loafers on Monday morning and even though it hadn't rained, Howard knew he would have to polish them again this Sunday before his sister Carol took him to church. He sits on the edge of his bed and pulls his socks up as high and tight as he can. Using the shoehorn that used to belong to his father, Howard slides the left loafer onto his foot. He flicks the tassels back and forth, giggling every time he sees the raw leather underneath.

"Howard! Howard, are you dressed yet?" Carol calls from downstairs.

"Yeah yeah sure."

"Then come down here and let me have look at you."

Howard carefully closes the door to his room, listening to make sure the bolt clicks shut and happily shuffles down the stairs to where Carol is waiting for him. She has Howard's blue windbreaker in her hand and already has her own coat on, even though it's summer and she really doesn't need one. Carol makes sure Howard has buttoned his shirt properly and zipped up his fly before getting him into his jacket.

"Did you remember to wash your hands after you peed?"

"Yeah yeah sure," Howard says, presenting his hands for inspection.

"Did you brush your teeth?"

Howard opens his mouth, revealing his half-dozen remaining teeth. Though yellow and stumpy, they are much better now that he is living with Carol. She brought him to the dentist, which hurt a lot and Howard had cried and cried all night . . . but the lady there was very nice. She had stroked his hand while the dentist jabbed and stabbed his mouth, and then she gave him a balloon when they were leaving. It all turned out okay in the end. Howard's whole mouth felt better the next day. And after his second visit, which also hurt a lot and made him cry, Carol let him eat candy again, but only one piece a day, and no gum.

Carol sniffs Howard's breath. She runs her hands through his thin silver hair and sighs. She doesn't look angry today. Most Friday mornings Carol looks angry. Howard knows it's not his fault, it's because she has to work late on Fridays. Carol has to make sure everyone is safe for the weekend and doesn't come back home until after suppertime. Howard eats cold food on Friday nights, but he doesn't mind.

Howard is happy that Carol isn't angry today. He almost giggles. Carol doesn't like it when he giggles, but sometimes he can't stop himself and he just keeps giggling and giggling and his stomach starts to hurt and he can't breathe and he hypers into the paper bag he keeps in the left-hand pocket of his windbreaker.

Howard doesn't giggle today because Carol, running her hand through his hair, doesn't look angry . . . she looks sad.

• • •

"Where's Mr. Krazy . . . Kraznyak . . . whatever his name is, the old guy in the floppy hat there who got a beef with the World?"

"He went out at ten sharp, like he do every morning." Luis doesn't look up from the sports section. What does Luis care if Ian, that big white ape who thinks he's such tough shit in his security guard suit, got a problem. Luis is far more concerned with Carlos Delgado's inexplicable slump. No doubt about it, the Jays need another bat in the order, give the big man a bit of protection.

"Do you know where he goes?"

"The fuck would I know that?"

"You talk to these wing nuts . . . you orderly guys."

Luis looks up from his paper. He does not like the way Ian called him an orderly guy. It's not a racist term per se and Luis knows this, but it sure as hell sounds like it coming out of Ian's fat Anglo/Scots mouth. The two men lock eyes. They hold it until Luis' pitch-black wins out over Ian's washy blue.

"Do you have the paperwork for his day pass?" Ian sighs, looking down at his fingers.

"No need, amigo, when they voluntaries like Mr.K." Luis is about to add something about how Ian, dumb fuck that he is, ought to know that, but he takes the high road. "Why? What's up?" He smiles and unfixes his stare. His hand almost touches Ian's forearm.

"Well . . . he's got a visitor."

"Who? Ms. Bleeding Heart the social worker?"

"No, a real visitor."

"No shit."

"Good-looking, too."

Luis puts down his paper. He drains what's left of his coffee, stands, stretches, puts his hand on Ian's shoulder and says, "Lead the way."

• • •

Howard stood outside the Chester subway station waving good-bye to Carol five minutes after she'd disappeared down the escalator before starting his walk downtown. It's an easy walk, in that all Howard has to do is walk west along Danforth and over the bridge where it becomes Bloor Street, which almost always makes Howard giggle. He keeps going until he gets to Yonge Street. He turns south on Yonge and heads into the heart of downtown. It would take most people about forty minutes, but Howard walks pretty fast. He likes to skip and jump over cracks in the sidewalk and usually there isn't much to see or do until Yonge Street anyhow.

Today there is something to see on the Danforth.

There are people on the sidewalks selling clothes and cooking food. There is a big banner across the middle of the street and there are no cars. Some people are wearing strange costumes and there is loud, funny music coming from most of the stores. A fat man with a big moustache, wearing a vest with jewels and beads sewn into it, slaps Howard on the back and gives him a small plastic cup with water in it, except that it smells like licorice.

Howard turns around and is transfixed by the huge red glass beads the moustache man wears over his heart.

"You know me, my friend," the man bellows. "Drinka! Drinka!"

Howard continues to stare at the beads. He reaches out to touch the biggest one.

The moustache man rears back laughing. "You like it, my friend? Too big for you I think! Ha Ha! Come, you drinka, it make you strong!" He guides the cup to Howard's lips. Howard is so caught up in fondling the big bead on the man's vest; he doesn't react until the ouzo hits his tongue.

Howard swallows and can't breathe. Tears come to his eyes. He begins to shake all over. The man with the moustache barks something in Greek and an old woman dressed in black bustles through the crowd with a glass of water.

"I sorry, my friend," the man says.

Howard takes the paper bag from his pocket and, with the old woman's help, puts it to his mouth. By the time Howard is calm enough to drink the water, the small crowd of onlookers has become re-engrossed in the street fair. The moustache man is back to spreading his good cheer and cheap ouzo. The old woman is the only one still paying any attention.

"You be okay," she whispers.

"Yeah yeah sure."

• • •

K. That's how he refers to himself and has since his youth. It sounds more like "Kya-chhhh" since his last stroke, the one that rendered his right hand into a jerking monstrosity, the one that had tortured his face into permanent, twitching discord. His thick Magyar accent, once thought so charming, further hampers his attempts to be understood.

Not that they could begin to comprehend him, even if they could be bothered to listen closely enough to decipher him. They being all of them; his ungrateful family (his awful niece and her bastard daughter), Jan and Lukas (so old now, they have to be told when they've shit themselves —

K should only be so lucky), the mongrel lackeys who mind the other enfeebled residents of the Queen Street facility (the old story of dogs and sheep), their clipboard-toting masters (fools and druggists), and then there is the average man in the street.

In the end, there is nothing quite so enraging as the man in the street, particularly these streets. They know nothing of life for they know nothing of survival. For them it is taken for granted, which one would think to be a noble attribute in a society until . . . until people self-actualize. Then they are revealed. They are the indulgent, self-centred cretins K has always known men to be. Moreover, they know nothing of suffering. K has survived and suffered. First fascism and racism, then war, famine, genocide, revolution, communism, exile, capitalism and now this state of physical disgrace. K survived by keeping himself fit and wary. From the age of ten, he did 100 push-ups, 100 sit-ups, 100 jumping jacks and 100 pull-ups every morning while others slept. There is no rest for K. He suffers even as he sleeps . . . with one eye open and a clenched fist.

K can no longer do his exercises. He no longer decides when his eye is to stay open or closed, when his fist will clench or when it will lie dead at his side. All K can do now is walk. And he does.

At ten sharp every morning K starts west along Queen Street to the Lushek Grocery where he buys his cigarettes, and on Thursdays, the local Hungarian newspaper. Mr. Lushek never speaks to him. He, at least, has some respect. On the days when Mrs. Lushek is behind the counter, K walks by cursing. The spasm in his hand and twitching in his eye become decidedly pronounced. Mrs. Lushek cannot resist sharing the intimate details of everyone's life with K, holding him under the spell of her cheap perfume and life-draining eyes. K will not be her captive, nor can he curse her, as he should, for fear of offending her husband, who, though a low-brow and henpecked fool, is at least tolerable in his persistent silence.

They are both in the store today.

He is stocking the shelves with jams and preserves from central Europe. She is in front of the counter displaying a loaf of bread to another grotesque matronly Magyar. K hesitates. He feels his hand, the whole arm below the elbow, move outside of his control. He turns on his heel, faster than an alley cat, and starts east towards downtown at an accelerated clip.

• • •

"Where the fuck is Elvis? I want my coffee."

"Lay off of Elvis. He's the King, man."

"He's a royal pain in the ass who won't go away."

"If he ain't here, Petey-boy, he can't go away."

"Always a wise-ass."

"I'll watch your stuff if you want to go to the Second Cup."

"Fuck you."

They both smile.

Luke, who had offered to watch Pete's wares, goes back to minding his own. Having already attached the eight 4'x 8' grids to his two rolling racks with an intricate array of bungee cords and securing the whole thing to a City of Toronto garbage can, he starts placing his T-shirts on the display. He has enough room for sixty shirts and has an additional 300 T-shirts, all extra-large 100% cotton, in two overstuffed hockey bags.

Pete, who sells knock-off designer watches, never trusts anyone to watch his stuff. It's not that he and Luke aren't buddies; Luke had saved him his spot this morning as he usually did. And it's not like Luke would steal from him. It's those fucking street kids. They'll swoop in, snag the whole display case and then be lost in the Eaton Centre crowd before Luke or anyone else can do anything about it. Also, quite frankly, what does Luke care? Luke's a good kid, really, but just a kid looking to make some bucks for college. He works for some other college kid, Stevie, who's so busy "empire building" he doesn't even notice the c-note Luke pulls off the top on a daily basis. It's probably worth it to let him steal. Luke's a real seller, you had to give him that.

Pete, on the other hand, is a man and his own boss, and in the end, he is just too lazy to close shop. It's too early for business to really get going, still, he doesn't want to have to pack the whole case up. He never should have started laying his watches out . . .

"They should have coffee vendors," Pete concludes.

"They do . . . just not here," Luke says, after a sip of his Jumbo French Roast. "I hear there's a guy with a coffee wagon outside Union Station."

"That's just a hot-dog guy with a thermos."

"It's a start."

"Where the fuck is Elvis, I ask you again?"

"What can I tell you, Petey-boy? Elvis is usually money."

· · ·

Carol puts down the magazine. Enough is enough. The guard has left his post unattended for at least the fifteen minutes Carol has been waiting. This is simply unacceptable behaviour. Slowly, methodically, and with great intent, she rises to her feet. She strides down the short hallway to the security door and very deliberately presses the buzzer repeatedly, holding it down for a four count each time.

Carol knows as well as anyone can that the anger she's experiencing is the only thing keeping her from becoming completely unglued. She also knows she's already missed her 9:30 interview, if you could call it that, with Mr. Krazny, but had hoped she might catch him on his way out. She even fancied the notion of taking him for a coffee, allowed herself to briefly imagine what it would be like to accompany him on one of his walks . . . but her oncologist had kept her waiting. It would seem that she's missed him completely. Carol sometimes doesn't know why she bothers . . . then she thinks of Mr. Krazny and her other clients, and where they'd be without her, and in the end, it always comes back to Howard. How will he manage after she's gone? Who will look after him? Carol, nine years younger than her brother, hadn't fully planned for that contingency. Their cousin Phyllis had made a vague promise, but that was nearly ten years ago when Carol was still trying to wrest Howard from the very institution that has kept her waiting these last fifteen minutes.

Through the metal caged window of the door she sees the big security guard, Ian, slowly make his way towards her. Then he stops, turns around and says something. He waits for a response and laughs when it comes. Carol is ready to press the buzzer again, but Ian turns, very quickly for a big man, and is at the door in two long strides.

"Sorry . . . nature called," Ian says, opening the door, taking the wind from Carol's sail.

· · ·

Howard is walking fast-fast with a high-pitched moan coming from his throat. He stumbles in the middle of the pedestrian bridge, scraping his hands on the hot concrete. He pops back to his feet and gags for air. He inhales deeply three times and doesn't have to cry. He starts walking again; slowly at first, watching his feet, counting his steps, pretending his hands don't hurt, then a bit faster and he can look up again.

Howard does not giggle as the Danforth turns into Bloor Street. There is a lump in his throat, a pocket of heavy air. Howard knows he is going to vomit and walks faster and faster until he is almost running. He is past the bridge and crosses Bloor Street in the middle between Jarvis and Church, instead of at the traffic light like Carol made him promise. There is no street fair here. The cars are going very fast and they honk at him. Howard stops in the middle of the road. A taxi driver screams out his window and Howard is moving again. The pulsing lump in his throat begins to transform into an open-mouthed cry. Howard doesn't make it all the way to Yonge. He runs down Church Street with his hands over his ears. The skinny men in tank tops outside the bank laugh as he runs past.

Howard turns into a little park that doesn't have a playground and throws up in the bushes. He sits cross-legged in the grass. He takes the paper bag from his windbreaker pocket and breathes into it three times. He feels much better and he didn't even get any vomit on his clothes. Howard grins and looks up. There are two men holding hands, standing over him, and looking down at him with concern.

"Are you okay, sweetheart?" the taller one asks.

"Yeah yeah sure," Howard says, springing to his feet and skipping past them. Howard would like to be holding somebody's hand.

• • •

There is something worse than the man in the street. There is the do-gooder. The trier. The one who always wants you to try this and try that. The one who says, "Try harder with your speech therapist, your physiotherapist, your psychiatrist."

She. That Woman. The social worker. She tries. She leans her whole awkward body in and squints her eyes to help her listen. She hears the words, but does not understand. Can never understand. That cow, with her big washed eyes, her plump little fingers always seeking K's shoulder, so obviously compensating for a life lived without physical love. She may know something of suffering, but she has never experienced passion.

"It's your anger," she says, time and again, as though she could begin to fathom. "The doctor said it could cause another aneurysm."

K had walked along Queen Street and turned north on Spadina, thus avoiding Kensington Market, where he'd sworn years ago never to return. Look at these people; these Chinese on the street, selling dried fish and vegetables, the same here as there. They are as they are. Is it love that drives them to build on each other like ants?

K turns onto Dundas Street and is confronted with a flyer stapled to an electric pole:

FLAMING NAZIS
WITH SPECIAL GUESTS GEOPOLED AND JOSH WAYNE HIGGINS
10 PM. THURS.-SAT. NIGHT AT LEE'S PALACE
$7 COVER

"FUCKINGNOREPEH K-K-K-KIZZZ!!" K screams at the poster. "WHO MANNY MILLION DIE, H-H-H-U-GGGN? PIGSHEETTER FACKBASTARD!" He takes a deep breath and looks as if he is going to stop, but his hand is arhythmically slapping his thigh and his eye won't open. K has no choice but, "ALL-V-V-V-V-AAAYS YOUFACKERS! FAAACKERS! YOU THINK KAKAKA I NONONO YOU? I KNOW! I KNOW! FAAAAAAA-CKERS . . . ."

When the torrent ends, the shaking and twitching stop with it. For a brief moment K feels like a real man again. A man controls his hands and feet. A man lives in his mind. The people are all looking away. None of them will look at him.

K continues east through Chinatown towards the centre of the city.

• • •

"Shit, Elvis where ya been? Poor Pete here almost had to close shop and get his own java? I mean, what's the world coming to, Elvis? Can you riddle me that?"

"Yeah yeah sure," Howard gleams. Luke is his friend. He always visits Luke first even though Luke sells T-shirts now and Howard doesn't like T-shirts, they don't shine. Luke used to sell gold chains and rings and he had silver and gold bracelets and a special cloth he used to make sure everything stayed shiny. Pete has a cloth he uses on his watches, but he won't let Howard help him.

"You alright, Elvis?"

"Yeah yeah sure."

"You look a little sick or something." Luke looks over and, noticing a customer mosey away from his neighbour's display case, says, "Hey Pete, got a sec?"

Pete, who still hasn't made a sale, snaps back, "What?"

"Elvis is here."

"Well, tell him to get me a Jumbo Kona and please, for the love of God and all that is holy, tell him to put the fucking cream and sugar on the side," Pete gives Luke his 1000-yard stare. "Oh . . . and can you cover it until I fleece my first?"

"I think Elvis is sick. You wanna take a look?"

"What am I, Trapper John?" Pete reluctantly comes out from behind his display case. He places his thumbs under Howard's eyes and pulls the loose skin of his eye-sockets into his cheeks. "He looks fine to me, but he's got liquor on his breath," Pete pronounces. "You been drinking, Elvis? You old scoundrel."

"Yeah yeah sure."

"Throw me a ten-spot," Pete demands over his shoulder.

Luke hands him a twenty.

"Elvis. Listen closely. Take this bill, go down to the Second Cup and get a Jumbo Kona for me and a Jumbo French Roast for Luke."

"Double double?"

"No. Now listen close. This is where it gets complicated. Are you listening?"

"Yeah yeah sure."

"You can get all the cream and sugar you like . . ."

"Double double?"

"As much as you like, just make sure they put it on the side. Do you understand? Make them give you a separate little baggie and you can put all the cream and sugar you like in the baggie . . . just don't put any in the coffee. You got that, Elvis? Because if you get it right, you get to keep the change."

"Yeah yeah sure." Howard snaps the bill from Pete's hand and trots off towards the Eaton Centre, skipping over the cracks and giggling "Double double" to himself.

"You're the King, Elvis," Luke calls after him.

•   •   •

Carol pulls her sweater tight over her shoulders and shivers. She listens to the sound of Ian's footsteps and those off Mr. Krazny's grandniece as they recede down the hall. Ian's bass thumps accompanied by Ms. Vargas' stiletto-heeled staccato. Carol hunches forward as another wave of shame breaks through her body. How could she be so unprofessional? How could she treat another human being that way?

"My name is Anya Vargas," the woman had said, her black eyes burning into Carol. "Mika Krazny is my mother's uncle."

"Yes." Carol offered her hand despite how uneasy the other woman's confidence and devastating beauty made her feel. "I'm Carol Flemming. I met your mother. She's a . . . very interesting woman. How is she?"

"She is dead," was the unblinking response.

Carol's hand snapped back, not that it was being taken. Ms. Vargas kept her hands folded tight to her midsection. She kept her elbows in so as not to touch anything.

This in no way mitigates Carol's sin. She had pulled back not because her hand had gone untaken, but because she was certain that touching the daughter of the dead woman would mean her own death. Moreover, Carol knows this striking young woman, this angel of death, can read her thoughts or kill with a blown kiss.

Carol had managed to collect herself enough to try to explain Mr. Krazny's progress: his physiotherapy went well at first, but some of the damage was permanent; the speech therapy, on the other hand, wasn't going so well. "He's not crazy," she had said. "Not really. Not yet. He's very angry though, and sometimes it's difficult to understand what he's saying. I think he finds this very frustrating."

Ms. Vargas seemed disinterested; she kept shifting in her impossible shoes, looking at her expensive watch, the floor, an opportunity to interrupt she didn't need.

Carol ran out of steam. She just didn't have it in her to explain the system, the paperwork, Mr. Krazny's case history. More disturbing to Carol was that she didn't have it in her to empathize with this woman. For this she couldn't forgive herself. She should have told her about Howard, broken that wall between them . . . at least she could have suggested home-care specialists or tried to explain Mr. Krazny's meds.

"Mr. Diaz will help you pack his belongings," is what she said.

Anya Vargas seemed satisfied and made to leave. She reached the door, turned back to Carol and said, "My mother was not an interesting woman. She was pedestrian, petty and mean."

Carol waited until she left before spitting up the cottage cheese and apricot she had had for breakfast.

• • •

"Pete, this is Fawn."

"Fawn?"

The young girl nestled into Luke's long body — your basic hippy-chick type, only wearing more metal than most of them — holds out a limp hand for Pete to shake? Kiss? Hold? What the fuck are you supposed to do when a woman holds her hand out like she's the Queen of England? Pete doesn't have a clue. He shuffles his feet and notices his eyes are shifting from side to side and he can't put a stop to either activity. Fucking Luke.

"Good to meet you," he finally stammers.

"Fawn here sells jewellery that she makes herself."

"Beady Hippy shit?" he says to Luke. "No offence," to Fawn.

"I would be offended if that's what I did."

"She speaks."

"She certainly does. Fawn, why don't you show Pete here your art?" Luke grins.

"Why? You think he's going to buy something?"

"I have no doubt, when Pete is a bit more liquid, he'll pick something out."

"Slow day, Pete?" Fawn asks, all full of concern. Christ, this chick is fiercely hot and Luke is all over her. Cocksucking, fucking kid.

"I saved a little space for Fawn on my other side. I have to take a grid down, but no worries," Luke explains, ushering Pete to the small, home-made wooden display case Fawn had propped up on an old card table. "It'll be sweet having you guys as my neighbours. I mean, like, *really* no worries."

Fawn pushes her way between the two male vendors. She opens her case to reveal a variety of objects; hair clips, necklaces, bracelets, earrings, finger rings and toe rings, all-moulded abstract female nudes. Fawn used white silver and high polished brass. She had alternately encrusted the erogenous zones of her women with amber and ruby glass beads.

"Oh, Christ," is Pete's all too audible first reaction.

Luke laughs and Howard comes trotting back with two large, regular coffees.

Double double.

•   •   •

How is it that the body begins to fail? A man can tell himself he is not like other men. Not that he is immortal, but that he can face death without facing the horror. He can rationalize his death as an event that will most likely occur in his sleep. Peaceable. Tranquil and without pain. Pain is reserved for the living. Pain, in the end, becomes a way of life, a sensation felt in every step, every breath and every thought.

At Bay Street, K decides to head south, circumnavigating the Eaton Centre if he should choose to turn again on Queen Street. He will land in the middle of the banking district if he keeps going straight. He needs to see the business hub of the nation today. He must listen in on the hollow men and let them crawl under his skin with their smug certainty, their corruption worn as just another fashion accessory.

When K dreams of the stroke that will kill him, as he often does, awake and asleep, if it does not occur in front of the Eaton Centre, at the Dundas doors, it happens at the corner of King and Bay. K will be walking by at his usual fast clip, seemingly intent on getting somewhere and .he'd see it — that certain look of complicity between two of these establishment crooks — and that would do it. That would be the outrage that bursts the ultimate blood vessel. K would end his life as he'd wished he'd lived it, in violent protest. His protest will not be verbal. K knows better than anyone the futility of the word. His protest will be in the form of his head, and under unbearable pressure from these many years, it will quite literally explode. He sees the culprits wiping his blood from their eyes, his scrambled, misfiring brains oozing onto their expensive shoes and they will know. They will know in their souls that K has died for their sins and one day so shall they!

"SHOWDE-DE-DEE-FACKERS!" K screams into the face of a young woman he'd been following since she'd left the bus station on Elizabeth Street.

The woman jumps back and swings her knapsack at him, missing by a good two feet.

"Get away from me, you fucking creep!" she yells.

"HAFACKER!" K yells back in triumph and turns on his heel in that quick-cat way of his.

• • •

"Why you wanna be fucking with me?" Luis says, flinging the inside door to Ian's cage open.

"Who's fucking with you?"

"I was just getting ready to make my move on that hotty and you bring in that bitch social worker so she can rain right on my parade. You fucking with my thing, man."

"Like you got a fucking chance, amigo." Ian smiles his big fat smile. He runs his finger down the length of his Billy club. "I think she's used to more man than you."

"Fuck you. White trash."

"Spic prick."

They lock eyes again.

"You want a donut?" Ian asks, nodding to the Tim Hortons' box on his desk.

"What the fuck?" Luis says, and takes a chocolate glaze from Ian's desk. "I don't think I can afford her anyways."

"I guess not."

Ian takes an old-fashion from the Tim Hortons' box. He smiles as he notices that there are still two chocolate-glazed left, as well as a Bavarian cream which they call Today's Special, despite it having been the special for at least the three years Ian had been shopping there. He'd eat the glazes after lunch. Maybe he'd even give another one to Luis. The special he'd eat around four; it's always the last to go.

"She's already done with Ms. Flemming."

"Who?"

"Your hotty. Mr. K's visitor."

"Yeah . . . whatever, man. Thanks for the donut . . . I should get back to the ward."

"That's right, amigo," Ian says, to push Luis' buttons. "Ms. Vargas wants you to go pack up Mr. Krazy's shit."

"Why didn't you say nothing?"

"She's been waiting for you in the hall five minutes," Ian grins through the frosting on his lips. "My bet is she's in a pretty pissy mood by now."

.   .   .

"I want the fucking change."

"Will you chill, Pete? It's my money, anyhow."

"Are you saying I'm not good for it?"

"I'm saying chill." Luke shoots him the corresponding incredulous look and sweeping hand gesture and wants to leave it at that.

"You did this on purpose."

"What are you talking about?"

"Are you telling me you didn't know Elvis would be all over your little girlfriend's porno hair clips?"

"So?"

"So? So, now we're never going to get rid of the little fucker."

"Don't speak ill of The King, man."

"That's not even his real name. Maybe your little flower girl would like to know why you call him Elvis. Now that I think of it, she'd probably love to hear him sing that song you taught him." Pete clears his throat and begins to sing, *"Ever since my baby left me, I found a new place to dwell, it's down at the end of lonely . . ."*

"You're a real head case, you know that?"

"I'm feelin' so lonesome I, I'm feelin' so lonesome I, I'm feelin' so lonesome . . ."

Luke is already at the other end of his monstrous T-shirt display by the time Pete is lonesome enough to die.

Howard, on the other hand, is completely enraptured.

As Pete had pointed out, Luke knew full well that the exceptional gleam Fawn brought to her work would be right up the King's alley. What he hadn't factored in was how the erotic component would affect the retarded man. Luke watches him fondling one of Fawn's pieces in one hand and grabbing at her arm with the other. The little man is all but rubbing himself up against her leg. He is repeating the mantra, "Shiny shiny girl. Yeah yeah sure."

Luke sighs and looks back over his shoulder. Pete is flashing him his special shit-eating grin.

• • •

It's all coming together. Yes. There is a sense of culmination. An air of finality. The police have erected their barricades. The world of the financial gods has been cut off to the ordinary man. There are forces in motion. K sees this clearly. There were the two men in sunglasses standing sentry on the southwest corner of Queen Street. Then the squad car that slowly drove past him twice. K does not have to be told that they are there for him. He can read the warning they are giving him. He will never give in, though. Never. Still, he must withdraw and wait for his moment.

K ducks into the south doors of the Eaton Centre. He almost never goes inside. His tormentors must know this. It is the only way to regain his freedom, but at such cost.

It is in here that people are at their worst. It is here that they connect to the unnatural world. They forsake poetry for convenience, love for goods and dreams for marketing schemes. In this place, you can clearly hear their insatiable need for banalities, smell the sex on them, become automatically attuned to their vile wants.

K darts through the early lunch crowd, sneering and twitching at those who don't give way to him as a matter of course. He stops briefly outside a music store hoping to be enraged once again by the Flaming Nazis. He sees no sign of them. K leaves the mall through the side doors leading onto Yonge Street, unsatisfied and free.

• • •

Maybe fine-fine Ms. Vargas needs him to get her a glass of water or wants directions someplace. Luis wants to say something, but can't find an opening. She looks through the window or at her watch. When she looks at him it's like he's not there. Is Vargas a Spanish name? Maybe he should ask her, he doubts it though. She says it with a hard "sh" sound at the end, and old Mr. Krazy ain't no Latino. But Holy Mother of God, the black eyes on that woman . . . she could make a man do anything. Luis likes her suit, too; black, V-cut, shortish form-fitting skirt, black silk (not nylon) on her legs and expensive-looking shoes.

"Excuse, senorita, you want I should pack these newspapers?"

"Pack everything," she says, still looking out the window.

Luis packs the newspapers. He tries to make some of it out, but they're all in some eastern European language he can't decipher. Besides the newspapers, his large suitcase (more than sufficient for K's minimal wardrobe) and a dozen books, mostly in the same eastern European language as the newspapers, there is nothing. No photographs. No Christmas cards.

"That's everything."

She doesn't say anything. She starts towards the elevator. Luis picks up the surprisingly heavy suitcase and the garbage bag full of old Magyar newspapers and stumbles after her. She stands by the elevator, one foot behind the other like a movie star. Luis waits at a discreet distance until the elevator arrives.

"Do you know that social worker?"

Luis looks away. He doesn't like talking about Ms. Carol-holier-than-the-Pope-in-Rome- Flemming. So once, when he first started working with these people, when he didn't know any better, Luis had slapped Howard around some. Howard was spazzing out. He couldn't stop giggling and kicking. He couldn't breathe. Luis got himself smashed in the shins ten, maybe fifteen times before he got in close enough to bring the freak down. Maybe he did give him a bit of an extra shot, a touch of revenge for all the kicking but . . .

But what Ms. Carol doesn't get is that Luis isn't like that. He doesn't like to hurt people. If a guy's got it coming, well Luis does have a sense of justice and likes the idea of the guy getting his. That doesn't make him some kind of sadist, does it? These poor people here don't have it coming. A guy doesn't go around picking on cripples and retards . . . at least not a guy Luis would associate with. He was sorry he had to hit Howard. He would take it back, even now, twelve years later, but Ms. Santa Carol de Toronto won't let him. She reminds him of it every time she looks at him.

"I don't really know her," Luis says.

They ride the elevator in silence.

•   •   •

"Luke, I don't know how to put this . . . but can you get your retard friend to leave me alone?"

"He likes you, Fawn."

"That isn't helping my business. He keeps touching my stuff."

"What two consenting adults choose to do in the middle of the street isn't any of my business."

Fawn takes a playful swat at Luke. He cuts a martial arts stance and puts that youthful twinkle in his eye.

"Will you be serious? How am I going to know if anyone is ever going to buy my stuff if your friend is there?"

"Look, Elvis likes shiny things. Give him something small and he'll probably fuck off, eventually."

"I already gave him a broach and I think he stole an anklet."

"Yeah, you gotta watch that. The King's got pretty sticky fingers." Luke strikes a thoughtful pose and waits for Fawn's agitation to rise a little closer to the surface. "Look, here's ten bucks. Give it to Elvis and he'll go get you a cup of coffee."

"Yeah yeah sure," she shoots back. "Then what?"

"Then we will have had ten Elvis-free minutes to decide how to get rid of him. Or we could just call it a day and go get a room."

"Luke!" It's Pete, who is trying to shoo Howard away with one hand and show, with the other hand, some very realistic-looking fake Cartier watches he keeps in a small leather case to a black guy from Detroit.

"I'm on it," Luke calls back. "Hey, Elvis. Fawn here would like some coffee. Wouldn't you like to get her a coffee?"

"Yeah yeah sure," The King says, taking Luke's money and giving Fawn a wet kiss on her cheek before skipping back into the Eaton Centre.

• • •

K is assaulted by the rank odour of rotted meat coming from the carts of the hot-dog sellers. They are the last in a long line of peddlers and urchins stretching all the way to Dundas Street. On a Saturday the line will continue past the centre doors almost all the way down to Queen Street. Next to the merchants of conglomerated animal parts is an old man selling cheap plastic sunglasses. K has seen this man before. A thousand times in a thousand places. His is the shaded face of the failed.

K looks back over his shoulder. An Eaton Centre security guard is just inside the doors saying something into his walkie-talkie and nodding at the garbled response. K quickly turns north along Yonge Street, along the line of street vendors, towards the corner with the greatest volume of pedestrian traffic in the city. K resists the urge to kick over a display of Christian books, forces himself not to be stopped by a novelty coffee mug with a cartoon image of one man, the current Premier, sodomizing another man, presumably the electorate.

"KERFACKIN SHEEETBRAIN!" K yelps out in passing.

He looks over his shoulder again. They are not following him and he is almost at the corner. He recognizes the shifty man with the watches in his coat and the huge T-shirt display. K pauses. He lets the real world flow around him; mothers dragging their children to buy new clothes, tourists purchasing proof of their journey, people of all races and classes converging on the food court for lunch, the retarded man in the banana yellow shirt and blue windbreaker being sent to buy coffee, the two good-looking young people who'd sent him ducking behind the enormous

T-shirt display, the boy's voracious eyes already loosening the girl's garments.

K stealthily makes his way to the end of the line of vendors, hoping to catch the young couple in the act, so he can give them a piece of his mind. He wants to soak them in his blood and bile. For today must be the day! These young people will be his death! K is stopped in his tracks. Before his very eyes is the unconscionable affront of a poorly made jewellery case containing gleaming silver, amber and ruby-red pornography.

K's right hand begins to tremble. He feels himself losing control of the left side of his face and the molten string of obscenities in his belly coming to a boil.

• • •

"This'll be epic. Here, just drag the other hockey bag over beside this one," Luke tells Fawn. He lugs the City of Toronto garbage can behind Pete and says, "Watch the trash for me, buddy. I'm going to close my tent for a few."

Pete, engaged in a nasty bit of haggling with a Rosedale Lady, isn't paying attention. Fawn has arranged the two T-shirt-stuffed hockey bags on the ground behind Luke's rolling rack and is standing on one of them. Luke climbs onto the other bag and starts to uncoil the bungee cords holding his grids in place. He kicks one of the rolling racks off to the side and pulls the freed grids around himself and Fawn.

"If you duck down for just a sec, I'll tie this end onto the other and voilà, we have our own little fort."

Fawn laughs and squats. Luke feels her hands working their way up his thighs as he hooks the bungee to the outside grid. When her hand brushes against him, shivers run up his spine. He pulls in the slack hard and fastens the other end.

Fawn wriggles her way up Luke's body and their lips meet. The kiss is deep and fused. They take their first pause, engage in their first mutual inhale. Before they can rejoin in earnest, they are startled by the sound of a man screaming in tongues. Fawn tenses and tries to bolt. Luke clutches her to him. He is smiling.

"What the hell is that?"

"That is . . . the Screamer."

"The Screamer?"

"He's one of my personal favourites. Little old guy with a floppy hat. He screams at anything that ticks him off — people with bad haircuts, lampposts, newspapers, garbage cans . . . he's got a real thing for skateboards. You never know what'll set him off. Half the time it's probably not what you think it is anyways. Sometimes, he just turns on his heel and follows people for no reason at all."

"This is a personal favourite?"

"Oh, for sure. It's like he's expressing my anger for me, for the whole world. The guy gets so righteously indignant, he's a total kick."

"If you say so."

"You want to go check him out?"

"I'm happy here."

"That's the right answer," Luke says, hoping to unhook, but happily finding that Fawn is not wearing a bra.

· · ·

Luis can't fucking believe it! No one told Ms. Vargas that Mr. Krazny goes out walking the streets. Ian didn't say anything. Luis gets that. Everything's a big fucking joke for that nazi ape. But Santa Carol? The bitch screwed the pooch on this one and who has to pay? Who's got to stand there in the middle of the street like a fucking idiot holding a suitcase and a garbage bag while Ms. Vargas starts going off about lawyers, closing down this mediaeval dungeon, making sure no one who worked here would ever work anywhere again?

Luis. That's who.

The way she went off made Luis feel two inches tall. He tried to tell her Mr. K always comes back around four, but she wouldn't let him. He mumbled something about calling her a taxi and slunk back inside.

Ian isn't in his cage. Chickenshit probably heard the fuss outside and is laughing his ass off somewhere. Luis jams his key in the lock and scrapes his knuckles trying to twist it out. He storms down the hall towards the elevators picturing himself yelling in Carol Flemming's face.

"You see? You see? It's not so fucking easy dealing with these fuck-ups? You see that you puta bitch? You're no better than me! You're no fucking better than me!"

He should go back up to the ward, check on the losers, make sure Tony and the new kid have them all medded-up and cooled down, but he hesitates at the elevator and back-tracks towards the visitor's lounge. He wants to run cold water over his bleeding knuckles and might as well use the only clean sink in the place.

The door to the visitors' washroom is ajar. No one is supposed to go in there without signing for the key. Luis thought he'd seen the key in Ian's cage. Well, maybe not. He hadn't really been looking for it, so it might not have been there.

He pushes the door open to check and sees Carol sitting on the edge on the toilet. She has her head in her hands. Her body is shaking. Her tears are flowing rivers.

"Mr. Diaz . . ."

"Luis . . . please Senora Flemming, call me Luis."

"Luis, I am going to die of cancer."

"I am very sorry."

Luis begins to cry.

•   •   •

"Double double," Howard giggles, putting Luke's change in the right-hand pocket of his windbreaker.

He doesn't care about the money.

The shiny chain is in that pocket and he likes to touch it. Fawn says you're supposed to put it around your foot. That's funny. It is too short to go around your neck. Howard had tried to put it around his neck as soon as he got on the escalator where Fawn and Luke couldn't see him. But he couldn't make it fit and it choked him and he coughed, so he put it back in his pocket.

It feels like a snake, smooth and cold with edges and with a naked woman instead of a head. Howard giggles and says, "Naked naked lady." He keeps giggling and has to sit down when he gets to the atrium. He takes out his paper bag, but doesn't need it. He removes the broach Fawn had given him from the breast pocket of his banana yellow shirt. The brooch is for Carol. It looks like her. Fawn called it primitive. Howard isn't sure what that means, but thinks it's nice. He imagines Carol pinning it to her sweater and then he can look at it when he hugs her and the one amber and two ruby eyes will look back at him and he can think about Fawn.

Fawn!

"Double double!" Howard jumps to his feet, remembering he is on a coffee mission and he can't let it get cold. He looks out the big window. She isn't there. He can't see Luke either and Pete, who's kind of mean anyhow, is talking to some customers. It looks funny, too. The corner is different and Howard doesn't know what to do. He looks again. The T-shirts aren't right and there is a man looking at the shiny things Fawn made. Howard starts to shake. He spills hot coffee onto his hand. It hurts. It hurts but Howard will not drop the cup. He taps his feet in place. He squints his eyes and holds his breath until he can breathe and see.

Howard runs through the atrium crowd, out the main doors and onto the corner of Yonge and Dundas. Everything is wrong. The garbage can is behind Pete and one of Luke's racks is on the ground beside it and a man is yelling at Fawn's beautiful jewels and he won't stop.

"NO NO NO NO NO!" Howard screams and grabs the yelling man in the floppy hat and spins him around. The man in the floppy hat locks eyes with him and Howard doesn't know what to do. He is crying, he can feel his hot tears. He can inhale and exhale and doesn't have to scream because it's okay, Howard knows this man. He can see him. K's face stops twitching, he is able to unclench his fist. They are both silent and still. There is nothing to say.

The silence is broken by the sound of Luke's T-shirt display crashing to the ground.

"Naked naked Fawn!" Howard yells.

She is on top of Luke and the two hockey bags, exposed to the world.

Howard can't breathe. He drops the styrofoam cup to the ground. It doesn't break, but rolls, spilling sweet, light coffee in an arc around his feet. Howard's fingers are frozen talons beating into his chest. His head is bobbing as though on a spring.

Howard turns and bolts into the middle of Dundas Street. K runs after him howling.

• • •

Luke sits on the curb. He has the coffee cup Howard had dropped in his hand. It is a hot summer afternoon, but he is shivering. He has a police blanket draped over his shoulders. Fawn took off quicker than a shot as soon as it happened. Pete is selling like gangbusters, the police line having diverted all pedestrian traffic right to his stand.

Luke is completely numb listening to the conversation the cop is having with the driver.

"If you'd like us to send you a copy," the cop is saying

"Of course I want a copy of the report! Do you have any idea how much it costs to replace the front fender of a Jag? Do you? This isn't a normal Jag either, my friend, this is the x-series, limited edition. You catching my drift, pal?"

"Just calm down, sir."

"I am calm. I am very calmly calling my attorney on my extremely calm cellular phone. I am going to ask him, with all due calmness, to get his placidly calm little ass down here as quickly and calmifically as he possibly can and then I will have him summarily write out a very uncalming complaint."

"I don't think there's any need for lawyers here, sir . . . unless you think I should be charging you with driving under the influence, speeding, reckless endangerment, vehicular homo—"

"First, there is already an attorney involved, he being me. Second, I have not been drinking and will eagerly take a breathalyser test. Thirdly, I was not speeding and, in fact, I had the right of way. Fourthly, this was clearly an instance of one crazy street person chasing another homeless maniac into traffic, and I can in no way be held liable or responsible for what ensued. Finally, after the collision, which has already caused me as yet unaccounted personal trauma, one of the said crazy street people tried to assault my person, arguably with intent to kill. I ask you once again, officer, what are you going to do about that?"

"Well sir, we have the man in custody."

"And?"

"Well, in cases like this . . . can I ask you something, sir?"

"What?"

"If you are an attorney, why do you have to call an attorney?"

"My field is property rights. Speaking of which, if you guys aren't too busy standing around trying to look busy, do me a personal favour and bust that jackass selling knock-off watches."

· · ·

Now K is denied his last perceived freedom.

The custody he is to be kept in is no longer voluntary. He will be within the confines of the same institution, of course, only in a smaller, more secure room, in a remoter, danker wing. After he is kept in seclusion for observation, he will be tossed in with the other maniacal dissidents. He will be drugged to virtual catalepsy and never be allowed to leave. K had seen it coming. Of this there can be no question. All the signs were there — Ms. Flemming missing their rendezvous, his decision not to buy cigarettes, the advertisements for filth and evil, the fornicating street youth and finally the murderous motorist. It was inevitable. K is furious with himself for having felt hopeful. Hopeful that today would be his day to die. But it was not his day to die. It was just another day to bear witness.

Why should K care about the retarded man in the yellow shirt? Granted, they were very much fellow-travellers. They had seen one another countless times as their worlds crossed in the streets. They were fellow travellers who never spoke of it. Yet there remains that moment, just after the retarded man had grabbed K by the shoulder and swung him around. That moment of silence. The retarded man had stopped his assault on K because he understood. Because he had looked into K and seen past the rage and paranoia to the root suffering, the stubborn will to survive and the sad need to die. Is that what led him to his end? Or was it the shock of seeing the young couple in *flagrante*?

K will ponder this question in the knowledge that he did not die. Cannot die.

This gentle man went in his stead so that K can continue to live in irony and at this advanced age, an age beyond reasonable death, find further reason to grieve.

ACKNOWLEDGEMENTS

My parents, sisters, Auntie and Uncle, eviler twin and his clan, the Plaws, even Dr. & Mr., the Callaghans, the McDevitts, Gervais, Warren, Valerie, Karen, Caroline, Tasha, Penny, Mary-Anne, Leila, Deb, Clara, Danielle, Esther, Harvey, Rose, Michel, Marie-Agnes, Joey, Gordon H., Gary, Steph, little Al, Robert, Paul, Meaghan, my students and teachers, Mircoscott, the boys at Harvard Paper and the countless others from whom I've stolen gesture, spirit and property.